Disciple

ALSO BY WALTER MOSLEY

LEONID McGILL MYSTERIES
All I Did Was Shoot My Man
When the Thrill Is Gone
Known to Evil
The Long Fall

EASY RAWLINS MYSTERIES
Blonde Faith
Cinnamon Kiss
Little Scarlet
Six Easy Pieces
Bad Boy Brawly Brown
A Little Yellow Dog
Black Betty
Gone Fishin'
White Butterfly
A Red Death
Devil in a Blue Dress

OTHER FICTION
The Tempest Tales
Diablerie
Killing Johnny Fry
The Gift of Fire / On the Head of a Pin
The Man in My Basement
Fear of the Dark

Fortunate Son
The Wave
Fear Itself
Futureland
Fearless Jones
Walkin' the Dog
Blue Light
Always Outnumbered, Always Outgunned
RL's Dream
47
The Right Mistake
The Last Days of Ptolemy the Grey

NONFICTION
Twelve Steps Toward Political Revelation
This Year You Write Your Novel
What Next: A Memoir Toward World Peace
Life Out of Context
Workin' on the Chain Gang

PLAYS
The Fall of Heaven

WALTER MOSLEY

CROSSTOWN TO OBLIVION

Disciple

A TOM DOHERTY ASSOCIATES BOOK • NEW YORK

In honor of PKD

ACKNOWLEDGMENTS

For my good friend Diane Houslin

Disciple

I OPENED MY EYES at three thirty on that Thursday morning. I was wide awake, fully conscious. It was as if I had never been asleep. The television was on with the volume turned low, tuned to a black-and-white foreign film that used English subtitles.

A well-endowed young woman was sitting bare breasted at a white vanity while a fully dressed man stood behind her. I thought it might be at the beginning of a sex scene but all they did was talk and talk, in French I think. I had trouble reading the subtitles because I couldn't see that far and I had yet to make the appointment with the eye doctor. After five minutes of watching the surprisingly sexless scene I turned off the TV with the remote and got up.

I went to the toilet to urinate and then to the sink to get a glass of water.

I stood in the kitchen corner of my living room/kitchen/dining room/library for a while, a little nauseous from the water hitting my empty stomach. I hated waking up early like that. By the time I got to work at nine I'd be exhausted, ready to go to sleep. But I wouldn't be able to go to sleep. There'd be a stack of slender pink sheets in my inbox and I'd have to enter every character perfectly because at the desk next to me Dora Martini was given a copy of the same pink sheets and we were expected to make identical entries.

We were what they called at Shiloh Statistics "data partners" or DPs. There were over thirty pairs of DPs in the big room where we worked. Our entries were compared by a system program and every answer that didn't agree was set aside. For each variant entry we were vetted by Hugo Velázquez. He would check our entries and the one who made the mistake would receive a mark, demerit. More than twenty-five marks in a week kept us from our weekly bonus. Three hundred or more marks in three months were grounds for termination.

I climbed the hardwood stairs to the small loft where I kept my personal computer. I intended to log on to one of the pornography Web sites to make up for the dashed expectations the foreign film had aroused.

I was already naked, I usually was at home. It didn't bother anybody to see a nude fat man lolling around the house because I lived alone. My mother would tell me that at my age, forty-two next month, I should at least have a girlfriend. I'd tell her to get off my back though secretly I agreed. Not many of the women I was interested in felt that they had much in common with a forty-two-year-old, balding, data entry clerk. I'm black too, African-American, whatever that means. I have a degree in poli sci from a small state college but that didn't do much for my career.

At least if I was white some young black woman might find me exotic. As it was no one seemed too interested and so I lived alone and kept a big plasma screen for my computer to watch pornography in the early or late hours of the day.

I turned on the computer and then connected with my

Internet provider. I was about to trawl the Net for sex sites
when I received an instant message.

Hogarth?

Nobody calls me that, not even my mother. My father,
Rhineking Tryman, named me Hogarth after his father.
And then, when I was only two, not old enough to understand, he abandoned my mother and me leaving her alone
and bitter and me with the worst name anyone could imagine. I kept saying back then, before the end of the world,
that I would change my name legally one day but I never
got around to it, just like I never got around to seeing an
ophthalmologist. It didn't matter much because I went by
the name of Trent. My bank checks said "Trent Tryman,"
that's what they called me at work. My mother was the
only living being who knew the name Hogarth.

Mom?

For a long while the screen remained inactive. It was as if
I had given the wrong answer and the instant messenger
logged off. I was about to start looking for Web sites answering to the phrase "well endowed women" when the reply came.

No. This person is Bron.

This person? Some nut was talking to me. But a nut who
knew the name I shared with no one.

Who is this?

Again a long wait, two minutes or more.

We are Bron. It is the name we have designated for this
communication. Are you Hogarth Tryman?

Nobody calls me Hogarth anymore. My name is Trent. Who are
you, Bron?

I am Bron.

Where are you from? How do you know me? Why are you
instant messaging me at a quarter to four in the morning?

I live outside the country. I know you because of my studies.
And I am communicating with you because you are to help me
alter things.

It was time for me to take a break on responding. Only
my mother knew my name and, even if someone else at
work or somewhere else found out what I was christened, I
didn't know anyone well enough to make jokes with them
in the wee hours of the morning. Bron was definitely weird.

Listen, man. I don't know who you are or what kind of mind
game you're playing but I don't want to communicate with you
or alter anything.

I am Bron. You are Hogarth Tryman. You must work with me.
I have proof.

Rather than arguing with this *Bron person* I logged off the Internet and called up my word processor.

I'd been composing a letter to Nancy Yee for the last eight months that was nowhere near completion. The letter was meant to be very long. We'd met at a company-wide retreat for the parent corporation of Shiloh Statistics, Info-Margins. The president of InfoMargins had decided that all employees that had more than seven years of service should be invited regardless of their position.

The retreat was held at a resort on Cape Cod. I liked Nancy very much but she had a boyfriend in Arizona. She had moved to Boston for her job and planned to break up with Leland (her beau) but didn't want to start anything with me until she had done the right thing by him.

She'd given me her address and said, "I know this is weird but I need the space. If you still want to talk to me later just write and I'll get back in touch within a few days."

She kissed me then. It was a good kiss, the first romantic kiss bestowed on me in over a year—way over a year. I came home the next day and started writing this letter to her. But I couldn't get the words right. I didn't want to sound too passionate but all I felt was hunger and passion. I wanted to leave New York and go to Boston to be with her but I knew that that would be too much to say.

Nancy had thick lips and an olive complexion. Her family was from Shanghai. Her great-grandparents came to San Francisco at the turn of the twentieth century and had kept their genes pretty pure since then. She didn't think herself pretty but I found her so. Her voice was filled with throaty humor and she was small, tiny almost. I've always been overlarge but I like small women; they make me feel like somebody important, I guess.

I composed long letters telling Nancy how attractive and smart and wonderful she was. I decided these were too effusive and deleted them one after the other. Then I tried little notes that said I liked her and it would be nice to get together sometime. But that showed none of my true feeling.

That Thursday morning at five to four I opened the document called "Dear Nancy" and started for the ninety-seventh time to write a letter that I could send.

Dear Nancy,

I remember you fondly when I think of those days we spent at the Conrad Resort on the Cape. I hope that you remember me and what we said. I'd like to see you. I hope this isn't too forward . . .

I stopped there, unhappy with the direction the letter was taking. It had been eight months. I had to say something about why I'd procrastinated for so long. And words like "fondly" made me seem like I came out of some old English novel and . . .

Hogarth?

I looked down at the program line but there was no indication that the system was connected to the Internet. Still the question came in an instant message box. There was a line provided for my response.

Bron? What the fuck are you doing on my computer? How are
you on it if I'm not online? I don't want to hear anything from
you. Just get off and leave me alone.

It is of course odd for you to hear from someone you don't know
and cannot accept. I need for you, friend Hogarth, to trust me
and so please I will give proof if you will just agree to test me.

What are you trying to prove?

That you and I should work together to alter things.

What things?

That will come later after you test me, friend Hogarth.

Test what?

Let me tell you something that no one else could know.
Something that may happen tomorrow for instance. An event.

Fine. Tell me something that you couldn't know that will happen
tomorrow.

Something *you* couldn't know, friend Hogarth. At 12:26 in the
afternoon a report will come from NASA about a meteorite
coming into view of the Earth. They think that it will strike
the moon but about that they are mistaken. It will have been
invisible until 12:26. It will be on all news channels and on the
radio. 12:26. Good-bye for now, friend Hogarth.

When he signed off (I had no idea how he'd signed on) I was suddenly tired, exhausted. The message boxes had disappeared and I couldn't think of anything to say to Nancy Yee. I went back downstairs and fell into my bed planning to get up in a few moments to go to Sasha's, the twenty-four-hour diner on the Westside Highway, for pancakes and apple-smoked bacon.

The next thing I knew the alarm was buzzing and the sun was shining into my eyes. It was 9:47 A.M.

I rushed on my clothes, skipping a shower and barely brushing my teeth. I raced out of the house and into the subway. I made it out of my apartment in less than eight minutes but I was still an hour and a half late for work.

"Ten thirty-eight, Trent," Hugo Velázquez said before I could even sit down.

"My mother had a fever last night," I told him. "I had to go out to Long Island City to sit up with her. I missed the train and then the subway had a police action."

I could have told him the truth but he wouldn't have cared.

The data entry room was populated by nearly all my fellow workers at that late hour. The crowded room was filled with the sound of clicking keyboards. The data enterers were almost invariably plugged into earphones, hunched over their ergonomic keyboards, and scowling at the small flat-panel screens.

The Data Entry Pen (as it was called by most of its denizens) was at least ten degrees warmer than elsewhere in the building because of the number of screens and cheap computers, bright lights and beating hearts. There were no offices or low cubicle dividers, just wall-to-wall gray plastic desktops offering just enough room for an in- and outbox, a keyboard, and a screen.

Of the sixty-odd data entry processors half turned over every year or so; college students and newlyweds, those who wanted to work but couldn't manage it and those who were in transition in the labor market. The rest of us were older and more stable: losers in anyone's book. We were men and women of all ages, races, sexual persuasions, religions, and political parties.

There were no windows in the Data Entry Pen. Lunch was forty-five minutes long conducted in three shifts. We used security cards to get in, or out. On top of protecting us from terrorists these cards also effectively clocked the time we spent away from the pen.

I sat down at my terminal and started entering single letter replies from the long and slender pink answer forms that Shiloh Statistics used for the people responding to questions that we data entry operators never saw. "T" or "F," one of the ABCs, sometimes there were numbers answering questions about sex habits or car preferences, products used or satisfaction with political officials.

"We put the caveman into the computer," Arnold Lessing, our boss and a senior vice president for InfoMargins, was fond of saying. He'd done stats on everyone from gang members to senators, from convicts to astronauts.

At the bottom of each pink sheet there was a code number. I entered this after listing all the individual answers separated by semicolons without an extra space. After the code I hit the enter key three times and the answers I entered were compared to Dora's . . . I usually made about twice as many mistakes as she did.

I WORKED THROUGH LUNCH and planned to stay late so that Hugo couldn't say that I was slacking off on top of being late. I often worked extra time anyway because Dora was also faster than I at entering data. I was usually running half an hour to an hour behind her at the end of the morning so working through lunch was a regular occurrence for me.

At three o'clock I was going full guns when I heard Dora say something fantastic to Miguel Corvessa, the mail clerk.

"They say it might hit the moon," Dora was telling the handsome young Mexican.

"Whoa," Miguel said. "You hear that, Trent? It's almost the end of the whole fuckin' world."

"A comet?" I asked.

"No," Dora didn't actually say *fool,* "it's a meteorite."

"What time?"

"Why?" Dora said. "Are you writing down all the meteorites in your journal?"

There was a healthy dislike between Dora and me. She was young, white, and very good-looking in a modern way. She most often sneered when looking at me. I don't dress all that well and I am old enough to be her father.

"Why don't you tell him, chica?" Miguel said.

Dora didn't like me but she was hot for the young Latino man. It was said that he was a fabulous dancer and Dora had made it known that she loved salsa.

"The Hubble telescope registered the thing at around twelve thirty," she said. "They said that it was moving in the shadow of the moon before that."

I had forgotten about Bron because I was late. Before falling asleep I dismissed the early morning electronic chat as an anomaly; maybe a high school friend who got my e-mail somewhere. But then, after the announcement of the meteorite appearing out of nowhere, I felt a chill between my shoulder blades.

"What's the matter with you, bro?" Miguel asked me.

"What do you mean?"

"You're shaking," Dora said with almost no distaste in her voice at all.

I turned my computer off and then back on again. After it had booted up I chose the Internet option rather than Stand-Alone. From there I went to the BBC news Web site to look up the latest news.

It was there:

Today the Hubble telescope detected a meteorite over a hundred feet in length hurtling out of darkness and headed, it seems, on a collision course with the moon. Scientists say that this is not an unusual event. Meteorites come in close proximity to the Earth and even enter our atmosphere with some regularity . . .

The article went on to describe how the celestial body avoided early identification because it was hidden in *shadows* cast by the Earth and the moon.

I sat there trying to dismiss the fear growing in my chest. There had to be some explanation.

. . . Astronomer Ivan Lingstrom told our BBC correspondent that he was shocked when he saw the meteorite register on his instrument panel. "At first I worried that it would collide with Earth," Lingstrom said. "I thought I should call my mother and tell her to say a prayer for me. It's rare that a meteorite of this size sneaks up on us. But I guess that there are many surprises out there in the universe . . ."

I wanted to get back to work, to normalcy, but Bron was the only thing on my mind. His proof seemed unassailable. But why would he need to prove anything to me? This man could see into the future, into space. I couldn't even find a girlfriend, a good job, pass the New York State driving exam.

"Mr. Tryman," Hugo Velázquez said.

He was a pompous little man who was partial to mute-colored suits with checkered vests. He was light skinned, from Honduras I think, and older than I was by a decade or more. Hugo didn't like people like me, whatever I was.

"Yeah?" I said distracted by the news and its ramifications.

"Are you online?"

"Uh-huh. There's this meteorite that no one saw but I—"

"It's against policy for data entry clerks to get online," the manager said. "You were told this. I gave you the memo by hand."

"Yeah . . . sorry."

"That is five marks."

The punishment focused my attention on the prissy floor manager. We'd known each other for eleven years. Eleven years of memos, marks, and ill-will. Here I had knowledge that even the BBC hadn't suspected before 12:26 and Hugo wanted to give me five demerits.

"How many marks in a dollar?" I asked him.

"What?"

"I wanna know how many German marks it takes to make up a dollar," I said. "Because when you finally add up to one you can take those marks and shove 'em up your ass."

"Oooo," Miguel said as if he had been shot.

Dora was staring at me, a grin of incredulity on her face.

"Mr. Tryman—" Hugo said.

"Listen, asshole," I said cutting off whatever company bullshit he was about to unload. "You don't have to worry. I know I'm fried. Fried and fired. I know."

His bottom lip was quivering. I think he wanted to hit me. When I stood up he took a step backward and Miguel cocked his shoulders getting ready to enjoy the fight.

I walked past Hugo using my security card for the last time on the locked door to the Data Entry Pen. When I got to the fourth-floor elevator I realized that I'd left my windbreaker hanging on the back of my chair but I didn't even care. I was never going back there. I hated my job and Hugo and Dora. Miguel was okay. He always treated me with respect. But I didn't give one damn about the rest of the people or the company. The whole damn place could blow up for all I cared.

IT WASN'T UNTIL I was on the street that I began to regret my adolescent behavior. I had barely enough money to make it through the month. Unemployment for just a week would put me in the red.

When I got home I found that the computer had turned itself on somehow and every five minutes for the previous two hours Bron had been writing my name.

Hey, Bron. I guess you made your proof.

Friend Hogarth, you have returned. I worried that you might have been hurt by some malevolent force or by accident on the street or subway. Where you live is so dangerous and you are so important.

Me? I'm just an unemployed jerk.

Your job is of no importance, friend Hogarth. You have vital works to accomplish. You and I will alter the world for the better. The prime life force on Earth will be saved by your exertions.

Me? I'm going to save civilization?

Just so. Your exertions will feed the Universal Mind.

You know, Bron, I think you might be cracked. The only thing I'll be doing for the foreseeable future is looking for a job.

For a while Bron was quiet. I had already begun to associate these periods of silence with thought. And I wasn't sure that it was human thought. For all I knew Bron was a very sophisticated AI system that had chosen me for some kind of corporate test.

Return to work tomorrow at 10:00 a.m. Your job will be
altered but you can still go to work.

Are you crazy?

Do meteorites come out from shadows of the past?

The humor and poetry of his reply took me off guard. I
wondered again why the disembodied intellect was interested in me.

What do you want from me, Bron?

On Saturday you will go to Michael's Pharmacy on Lexington,
retrieve a prescription, take a cab, and go to a concert at
Alice Tully Hall at the place called Lincoln Center.

Bron said much more. He went over every action he
wanted me to take detail by detail. A lot of it I wondered
about but no matter what I found odd or questionable my
mind kept drifting back to that meteorite. He had accu-
rately predicted the future. There was something amazing
and definitely disturbing about Bron. But he was just a voice
on the Internet, not any kind of real threat.

I wanted to find out more.

We messaged each other until almost midnight. At first
we talked about the job Bron wanted me to do. I was to "say
a few kind words" to two men. One was a Bangladeshi cabdriver named M. D. Amir and the other was young man
from Ohio who was running for the Senate seat there. The

cabdriver would have a mild communicable infection so I was to take an antibiotic to counteract the possible effects.

The things he wanted me to do were not exactly criminal but certainly odd. In the world of post-9/11 I had no intention of going between Muslim foreigners and politicians even if I wasn't passing off or giving out information. In the world of antiterrorism you could be stripped of your rights for just being stupid. There was no way I planned to do what Bron asked of me. But I wanted to hear him out. I wanted to discover how he knew about that meteorite. I had never been privy to something before they even knew about it on TV.

After the business at hand Bron asked me about my ninety-seven aborted letters to Nancy Yee. He had been monitoring my computer for seventeen months. He knew all of my porn sites, online video games, music downloads, and even the documents I'd written.

She will come to you if you ask her to.

You don't know what you're talking about, Bron.

I WENT TO BED that night without turning on the television. I couldn't remember the last time I'd done that. Television was my sleeping pill, my soporific, my constant friend. I always watched TV to go to sleep . . . but not that night. I lay there thinking about my new electronic pen pal. He knew more about me than anyone else, even my mother.

I woke up early, about seven or so.

I was unemployed so there was none of the usual rush. I

made coffee, sat down at my little dining table, and started reading a novel called *Night Man*. I'd had the book for months. Nancy Yee had given it to me at the retreat on the Cape. She said that she thought I would like it. I wanted to start reading again but between my TV shows, porn, anime, porn anime, my job, and music from any time before 1985 (I especially liked sixties British pop) I didn't have much time to read. That day, however, I had no previous engagements so I opened the book to page one.

Nancy was right—I liked the story very much. It was about a lonely man who shunned the daylight. He worked and played only in the nighttime hours of New York. He lived in a room three stories below ground so that no one knew where he was and daylight could never reach him.

At one point I came across the word "susurration." I didn't know what it meant so I considered going up to my loft nook to look it up in the online dictionary. But I decided not to because I knew that Bron would be waiting for me and Bron was beginning to make me feel uncomfortable.

He wouldn't explain how he knew about the meteorite or my given name or how he could communicate with my computer even when I wasn't online. He kept fobbing me off, saying that we should work together first to see how we might disseminate information in our world-altering adventures.

I was sure that he was fooling me somehow. It was probably some stupid prankster, maybe one of Dora's boyfriends, sitting at home and jacking into my system to make a dupe out of me.

I got so angry that I couldn't read anymore.

I didn't want to watch TV or listen to The Kinks or even masturbate. So I went to the closet, got out my dark blue suit, a light blue shirt, and black leather shoes. I got dressed as well as a bulbous and bald man of middle age can hope to, then I went down into the street and hailed a cab to go to the workplace that I'd already quit.

I had $1,247 in the bank; $950 of it earmarked for rent. I felt the growing pressure in the back of my mind about rent and food and the bills.

When Bron had said that my job would still be there I dismissed the thought. Predicting the meteorite was a trick or a fluke. But he was right no matter what I suspected. And so I decided to give him a real test. I'd see if he actually managed to get my job back.

They'd probably laugh at me down at Shiloh but if they wondered why I was there I'd just tell them that I'd come to get my windbreaker before taking an extended trip to Europe to get my head straight. I'd tell them that I had twelve thousand in savings and that I deserved a good vacation.

I WAS MILDLY SURPRISED when my key card still opened the pen door. It was company policy to remove from the security database anyone who retired, quit, or got fired from Shiloh. After all who wants a disgruntled ex-employee with a key to the front door?

When I came into the pen Dora was looking up from her terminal. When she saw me she turned away quickly. Miguel passed by. He looked both ways to make sure that he wasn't being watched then winked at me.

I went up to Miguel, my one friend at Shiloh, and asked, "Why's Dora acting so weird?"

"You, dog," he replied. Then he touched my shoulder and winked again.

"Mr. Tryman," a man said in a deferential tone.

I had to turn and look before I could identify the speaker as Hugo.

"Hey," I said waiting to see if Bron had pulled it off.

I felt like an idiot believing some crazy person on the Internet. I should never have come back to work. Hugo would sneer at me hoping that I was about to beg him for another chance.

And the truth was I was ready to beg him. I needed that job. Maybe this was Bron's plan. He'd get me to go back to work and then it was simple logic that we'd talk about my actions the day before.

"We got the message in the late afternoon, after you left . . . sir," Hugo said. *Sir?*

"I called upstairs," he added. "They told me that I was to escort you."

"Escort me? If you want me to leave all you have to do is ask. I just came to get my windbreaker. I'm going to Europe . . ."

Hugo smiled awkwardly and took me by the arm. He led me through his office and down the inner hall. Both places were usually off-limits to the data entry operators. At the end of this hall of red linoleum we went through a pair of ornately carved pine doors and came to an elevator. Hugo had to use a key to operate the mechanism. We got in and traveled from floor four to seventy-six.

Hugo led me down another long hall. This corridor was

much fancier with floors of marble tiles and double-sized doors of knotty hardwood. The extra-wide passage brought us to a huge hall with forty-foot ceilings and two opposite walls of amber-tinted glass infusing the room with filtered sunlight that was both warm and lush.

The chamber was mostly empty, dominated by those windows and a vast gray and green marble floor. This was the Great Hall where InfoMargins and other wealthy companies and individuals put on fabulous New York affairs. Almost every week there was a photograph on Page Six about the movie stars and billionaires at some event in the Great Hall.

Few of the four thousand employees of Shiloh had ever been allowed this far into the company.

"You been here before?" I asked Hugo as we made our way like two dark beetles across the marble expanse.

"No." He was so awed that he forgot to say "sir."

"Then how come we're here now?"

"They told me to," he said like a child who knew he was in trouble.

When we reached a towering double door on the opposite wall a man in a gray suit stepped out to meet us. He had black hair and oceanic blue eyes. Fifty and fit, he had a mien that informed anyone not blind that he was their superior.

"Here we are, Mr. Fitzhew," Hugo stammered.

This superior man nodded deferentially to me and then addressed Hugo.

"Take him in."

"Me?" Hugo said.

"That's what he asked for."

The double doors opened upon a hallway even wider

that the one that led to the Great Hall. There were no doors along the side, just one painting after another—from the Renaissance, by the looks of them. I wondered if they were originals.

After two hundred feet or so we came to a pearl-and-aqua–colored door.

Hugo hesitated a moment, obviously wondering if he should knock. He finally decided to push the door open. After doing so he ushered me in before him.

It was the largest and most opulent office I'd seen at Shiloh but when I saw the woman behind the desk I knew that I had only made it to the receptionist's post.

The woman was gorgeous. Brunette and tall with the kind of figure they exalt in upscale men's magazines. She wore a hard-finished coral dress that would have fit in at any cocktail party or cotillion. I'd seen her before in the building. Even when she looked in my direction she only saw the other side.

"Hello, Mr. Tryman," she said in the friendliest voice and rising like some pink naked goddess from a seashell.

I tried to answer but my heart was in the middle of doing a somersault. I couldn't even count the number of nights I had gone to bed thinking about her.

"I'm Trina," she said. "Anything you need, day or night, and I will be there."

I tried to think how much work a practical joke like this would take.

Trina walked to another large set of doors that stood behind her and flung them outward in an tastefully understated gesture of a vassal making way for her lord.

Hugo took me by the arm but I balked.

"What the hell's goin' on here, Hugo? Yesterday you were on my ass for lookin' at a news story online."

"I'm very sorry about that, sir," Hugo said. "I hope that you'll accept my apology."

"What does Lessing want with me?"

"Mr. Lessing is gone," Hugo said ominously.

"Gone where?"

"He's been transferred to DynoBytes in Fresno. I, I thought you knew."

"Knew what?"

"You've been promoted to Mr. Lessing's position," Trina said. "From now on you're in charge of Shiloh Statistics."

I heard the words and understood each and every one of them. But their meaning was something completely different than what the beautiful assistant was trying to communicate. All I could think about was Bron and the insane level of power he exhibited.

Hugo Velázquez guided me into the mahogany, maroon, and in all other ways well-appointed office. The desk was the size of king-sized bed. Two antique wide-bottomed, red-lacquered Chinese thrones were set before it for visitors and guests. A lush, rose-colored sofa was off to the left crouching like a pink lion before towering bookcases filled with hardback tomes and encased in glass. The window looking down on Broad Street was at least fourteen feet high and twice that in width.

I heard the door close behind me. Trina had left, sealing us in.

"Are you fuckin' with me, Hugo?"

The poor Honduran didn't know what to say.

"Am I gonna sit down here and then Lessing's gonna come in and have me arrested?"

"No, sir. No. The word came down yesterday. You are the new vice president in charge of operations." The look on Hugo's face was both confused and humble.

My heart was thumping like an agitated beaver tail. I made it to the modern, egg-shaped chair behind the huge desk and sat down. I was stunned. I could see in his eyes that Hugo was just as dumbfounded.

Slowly the reality settled in on me. I was the boss, the big man. My whole life I had fantasized about this happening. I'd be powerful and rich and respected. Beautiful women would look at me and smile no matter how fat or ugly I was.

But I hadn't done anything to earn this position, this power.

"Who called to tell you about my promotion?" I asked Hugo.

"President Mack called Mr. Lessing personally yesterday afternoon after you'd gone home."

"Justin Mack?"

"Yes. He told Mr. Lessing to be on the next plane to San Jose."

How had Bron done it? Justin Mack was on all the Fortune 500 lists. Among the biggest companies, the richest men, the greatest innovations. Mack was a throwback to the days of Carnegie, Frick, Morgan, and Ford. As important as Arnold Lessing liked to pretend he was I knew that he had never actually talked to Mack. An article I read in *Business Elite* magazine had said that the reclusive billionaire only communicated with his staff (which included sixteen vice presidents) through his confidential assistant Lisa Starfield.

Mack's assistant was the only connection between Shiloh and InfoMargins, and she communicated mainly by e-mail and only now and again by phone.

"Mr. Tryman?"

Mister.

"Yes, Hugo."

"May I go, sir?"

"Yesterday you threatened to give me five demerits for getting online," I said, couldn't help saying it.

Hugo didn't answer. He made his hands into useless balls and brought his thumbnails together. Velázquez was older than I. He'd worked for Shiloh since its beginnings more than thirty years before when it was Alhambra Testing. Over the years it had been part of Acme Academics, Scholastic Partners, the Fremont Board of Testing, and finally Shiloh Statistics under Justin Mack's InfoMargins. Hugo had absolutely no skills outside of those specially grown in the culture of this testing turned statistical company. He was like a wrangler for some nearly extinct creature; an expert blacksmith in the age of plastic.

If he lost that job he wouldn't be able to find decent employment anywhere. He was fifty-three and nearly useless. Even grocery stores and fast-food hamburger joints would think twice before hiring him. He had no technical skills outside of those associated with the systems used to embarrass and humiliate his staff.

As I had these thoughts I stared at the man I'd finally stood up to just yesterday. It was a source of pride that I talked back *before* I was elevated above him. I wondered if I asked him to shove a dollar up his ass now would he do it.

Luckily for him I didn't want to find out.

"Go on back to your duties, Hugo. I'll call you if I need you."

He sighed in relief and went out of my new office door, closing it as he went.

I swiveled around in the private cave made by my ecru-colored egg-shaped chair and looked out on lower Manhattan. The World Trade Center was gone but downtown was still magnificent. On this high floor Lessing had a corner office that allowed views of New Jersey, Staten Island, and Brooklyn. I saw both the Verrazano and the Brooklyn bridges.

I didn't know what my salary would be but I was willing to bet it was above the $1,038.86 I got every two weeks for data entry. I should have been happy but all I wanted to do was run. There had to be something wrong with me being there. Either there had been a mistake or worse, I was being set up for some kind of crime that was going to get me into serious trouble.

I was in no way qualified to be the boss of some big-time data disseminating firm. I was a forty-two-year old data entry clerk who could look forward to the bankruptcy of Social Security; a foot soldier in the class wars of America worn down and ultimately crushed by men like Justin Mack. At that moment I preferred the ignominy of poverty and unemployment to the spotlight of the sun shining down on me through that high window.

I turned back to the desk intent on calling Trina to tell

her that I was resigning my position. I would have done it too if it weren't for the computer terminal on the left side of my broad desk.

Friend Hogarth.

Bron?

I told you that you would not be fired.

How did you do this?

I own InfoMargins the holding company of your firm.

I thought our company was American owned.

That term has little to do with me. Now that you have a job you can work with me to alter things.

Justin Mack owns InfoMargins.

Nothing is as it seems, friend Hogarth. Nothing in the world that human beings believe in is really what exists. There was no primal atom, no Big Bang. There is no space as such. Life is not unique. There is no Not God.

The immensity of the implications Bron set forth unmoored me from more petty concerns. For the moment I forgot my reservations about work. It was dawning on me that I knew someone somewhere in the virtual world who at least pretended to be my guardian angel. But his knowledge

was also a terrible thing to me. I was too small, too insignificant to be on the playing field with him. I watched cartoons and played video games where I popped little
like-colored balloons to gather meaningless points over and
over like a dog chasing his own tail.

Bron?

Yes, friend Hogarth?

I don't understand what's happening. I mean the things you
see, the things you do are so much beyond me. My life is
nothing in this world. I have no money. I don't know anything
worth a damn. Why are you doing all this for me?

I have told you already, friend Hogarth. You and I are to alter
the world together.

I don't know what that's supposed to mean but even if
I did you're the one who has the power. Not me. You own
InfoMargins. You see into tomorrow and know things that no
one else even suspects. There must be better allies or agents
than me.

For a time then the computer screen was still. Over the
last thirty-six hours or so I had come to understand that this
wasn't uncertainty on the part of Bron but consideration.
My questions got down to the core of his business with
me. I sat there staring at the eighteen-inch LCD monitor
as if it were the face of someone who I had not yet classified
as friend or foe.

Time, friend Hogarth, exists in discrete moments of being,
subject, among other things, to intelligent awareness. For all
forms of awareness everywhere in the universe there is a now
and a then. But for some of us the now comes in larger pieces
and the then in an endless string of potentials, possibilities.
A moment for me is akin to many months for you. I perceive
days, weeks, and even longer as I look around me. I see you
eating what you call a rib eye steak but you won't eat it until
what is for you next Tuesday. I see that you are the only one
who can help me save what is essential for the well-being of
Earth. I see in you the strength and desire that we will need to
save so many trillions of trillions souls.

If you see what I'm going to do then why even talk to me? I will
do whatever it is you see anyway.

I see many things at once like the complex eyes of one of your
insects. I see you eating steak, watching naked women on the
computer screen, lying dead on Broad Street after shooting
innocent pedestrians. I see possibilities. I am here to help
guide those possibilities.

In order to do what?

To save what you call civilization, life, the Supreme itself.

I had no response to his wild claims and he had no more
to add.

———

OUTSIDE THE WINDOW I saw a flimsy white plastic bag rising on the currents between skyscrapers. Hundreds of feet above the ground the cheap sack was for the moment exalted, soaring. It was then that I succumbed, albeit momentarily, to defeat. Bron had mastered me with his insights and his power, his reach into the heart of a world that I had not even suspected a day ago. I was that hapless bag. *But who knows?* I thought. Maybe I would find just the right series of breezes and stay aloft for weeks, years. All things are possible.

This notion struck me rather hard. I realized that I might have only moments before I crashed to Earth, a meteorite from a shadow or a gust of wind out of nowhere.

"YES, MR. TRYMAN?" Trina said hopefully into the intercom.

"Could you come in here please?"

Ten seconds later she was there in front of my desk, possibly the most beautiful woman who had ever noticed my existence.

"Yes, sir?"

"Do I have any money?" I asked. "Cash I can get my hands on?"

"Yes, sir." She went to a bookshelf on the wall to the left of my desk. There were all kinds of books there. She slid the glass casing aside and pulled on a heavy looking bookend in the shape of a phallus. The bookshelf swung outward as a door and a gleaming metal safe larger than a restaurant refrigerator came into view.

Trina turned to look at me.

"I don't have the combination," she said.

I typed the question into the message line on my computer and Bron answered swiftly giving me the twenty-one-digit code. I scribbled it down and went to the keypad at the side of the silvery metal door. Trina turned away, I entered the number, and the door slid aside revealing a room filled with black binders, boxes of machinery, and one shelf piled with stacks of hundred-dollar bills.

"He can just take this money when he needs it?" I asked.

"You can."

There was adulation in her tone. Trina was moved by the power I had. The eyes that had looked through me for so many mornings and afternoons now took me in as if I were a rare jewel, a fat deity.

"What's your last name, Trina?"

"Mallory."

"Well, Miss Mallory. Thank you. That'll be all for now."

She nodded and smiled and hurried from the room as if she were on a mission of great importance.

I took six thousand dollars from the shelf and closed the safe.

Something was wrong. Something was right. There was also something that I should have been doing but I had no idea what it was. And there was no one I could ask for advice. Anything I said might get back to Bron. And no one I spoke to would believe what I had experienced. So I'd have to be like that plastic bag, floating on air until I landed or crashed or maybe drifted out to sea.

———

I WENT TO CHEZ MAURICE FOR LUNCH. Trina Mallory made the reservation. I had pork simmered in a red wine and mushroom sauce with ramps, fingerling potatoes, and a salad in a port-based dressing that was the best I'd ever tasted. I had a snifter of cognac and plain vanilla ice cream for dessert, even though it was not on the menu. The liquor helped me more than anything.

Who was Bron? What was he? The alcohol allowed me to consider these questions impartially. I could see plainly that I had no immediate access to answers and that none would come from any means available to me. I had to play along, to go with him in that taxi, to that concert.

*T*HAT NIGHT MY BUZZER RANG.

"Hello?"

"Hi," a young woman's voice said. "Is this Hogarth Try-man?"

"Who is this?"

"I'm Mink and my friend here is Shawna," she said as if I had a hidden camera and was looking at them.

"Hi," another girl's voice squealed.

"Bron sent us to keep you company tonight," Mink said.

My first impulse was to send them away. I didn't know them. I hadn't asked for them. The cognac had given me a headache. But maybe these women had spoken to Bron, maybe they could tell me something . . .

I hadn't said anything since "Who is this?" and so the buzzer sounded again.

"Yeah," I said.

"Just let us come up to your door, Hoagy," Mink said.

"Look at us through the peephole and then make up your mind."

I pushed the button and then pressed my eye against the peephole.

Two young women, one Asian and one black, came up the stairs looking like lovely apparitions in the distorted glass. They were wearing pink and gray raincoats, smiling and petite, beautiful and trashy. The black girl took off the Asian's raincoat revealing the completely naked young woman standing boldly in the hall.

"You can't open this door," I said aloud to myself even as I threw the locks open.

"You don't know a thing about these women," I said, turning the knob.

The black girl came in first followed by the other. While the Asian call girl closed the door the other one dropped her raincoat to the floor. Her skin was blacker than most African-Americans' skin. Her tilted, almond-shaped eyes didn't have our suspicion or our fear.

"I'm Mink," the Asian said. She put her foot on the wall revealing her well trimmed sex. "It's dirty, Hoagy. Get on your knees and clean it out with your tongue."

It was a tableau from a scene I had watched over and over again on a Web site from Spain. I knew that when I got down on my knees that the black woman would rip open my pants and grab my balls while I strained under Mink.

I HAD NEVER HAD SEX like that but I'd always wanted it. Odd that the fantasy is somehow more satisfying; satisfying but nothing like real. I think the drinks they gave me had drugs in them. My erection lasted throughout the night. I'd pass out from time to time but Mink or Shawna would pour ice-cold water on me and the sex would start again.

When I woke up in the morning Mink and Shawna were gone. It was nearly one in the afternoon. I lurched into the bedroom and got dressed in casual clothes. I hurried for the door but then remembered Bron.

He was waiting for me: a one-word interrogative.

Hogarth?

Why'd you send those girls?

Because you always wanted to but never did.

There's nothing wrong with what I'm about to do, right, Bron?

You are about to become a hero to the peoples of infinity.

Am I going to die?

One day. Not today.

Do you know when I'm going to die?

Follow our plan exactly, friend Hogarth. Get the medicine. Take it before you enter the theater. Say what we went over to Mr. Amir and Mr. Ontell. Shake their hands and come home.

How can any of this alter anything?

A gnat landing on a child's nose might avert a war or herald
the slaughter millions.

I TOLD THE WAIFLIKE BLOND-HAIRED pharmacist's assistant that I was Matt Honoree. She gave me a stapled-shut
white bag. Outside I tore the bag open revealing an amber
medicine bottle that had only one turquoise pill in it. The
physician who prescribed the pill was a Dr. Max Bron.

From the pharmacy I walked to the entrance of the Pied-
mont Hotel where at three sixteen I raised my hand and a
cab stopped.

The cabbie's nameplate read M. D. Amir as Bron had predicted. I was getting used to my e-friend's prescience.

"I'm not going far," I told him. "Just right over to the
Plaza."

"That's okay," Amir told me. "I just picked up a man at
JFK. He came all the way from Chad."

"You from Bangladesh?" I asked the young brown-skinned
man.

"Yes," he said with enthusiasm. "Have you been?"

"No but I hear that it is a beautiful country filled with
people who have sophistication and culture."

This seemed to make the young man very happy. He told
me that he loved his homeland and hoped to make enough
money one day to go back there and buy a farm large enough
to support him and his loved ones.

"America is okay," he said. "But there is no heart here.
Only money and work."

I was thinking that I had been trying to keep a savings account growing for the first eighteen years I'd been working

and on my own. It was my dream to buy a condo with a view of the Hudson. True happiness came later for me when I gave up that dream and took over my mother's rent-controlled apartment.

"I think I'd like to visit your country one day, Mr. Amir," I said trying to compliment the young man as Bron asked me to. "Maybe by the time I get there you'll have come back and become a great man."

"Thanks to God," he said swaying slightly in his seat.

I didn't see anything wrong with being kind and friendly to the young cabbie. There was nothing criminal about being nice.

If Bron's notion that a few friendly words were like a gnat on the nose of a child and his intentions were to save life then I was gently doing good deeds; a small price for the nicest office on the seventy-sixth floor.

For a while I wondered if I was defusing or creating a terrorist but thinking about it I realized that the young man didn't seem to have any hatred or fanaticism to him. He was just a kid living out an adventure with the wish to go home.

When we got to the hotel and I paid him over the seat.

He grinned at me. His eyes were bright. He shook my hand and nodded.

"Come see me in Bangladesh, my friend," he said.

"I will."

I WENT TO THE HOTEL BAR and ordered cognac. I had more than five thousand dollars in my pocket and no one to answer to. The drink felt good. It helped me to think.

I was wondering how I got to that hotel in the late afternoon. Bron just popped in when I had awoken unpredictably . . . But maybe my insomnia *was* predictable. He could see into the shadows of space, maybe he could see me watching that silly French film, drinking water too fast, walking up the stairs.

I hadn't called my mother in three weeks. I was mad at her about something but I had forgotten what. I was thinking about my mother because I was trying to come up with someone I could talk to about these crazy events with Bron. But Mom wouldn't have understod and I had no close friends.

Maybe Bron knew these things too.

He had implied that he wasn't human, that he lived where time occurred in larger pieces. But probably he was just some New Age fanatic.

Thinking about time I looked at my watch and saw that it was after five. I was fourteen minutes late for my departure.

I ran out of the bar and into the street where I hailed a cab. I told him I'd give him an extra twenty dollars if he hurried. Because of that I was only twelve minutes behind time picking up the ticket held under the name Joe Lion.

I rushed into the hall and up to my seat breathless and afraid that Bron would turn against me. I didn't want to give up my new job just as much as I feared my inexplicable *luck*. I sat there next to an empty seat looking at the wide blue curtain before me.

I was in the middle front row in the balcony. The cognac soothed me. The memories of Mink and Shawna jittered playfully in my nerves.

"Bron told us what you needed, Hoagy," Shawna had whispered in my ear as she raked her fingernails across my nipples. "He said that you needed to feel it."

"Excuse me, sir," a man said.

I looked up to see a young white guy in a suit that cost three times what mine did. He was smiling but didn't mean it.

"Yes?"

"I'm going to have to ask you to change seats."

"Why's that?"

"We need it."

"'We' who?" I asked. "I mean, no. I bought my ticket and now I'm gonna see my show."

I resented this MF coming up and expecting me to move when I was a paying customer just like everybody else. Or, at least, someone had paid for the ticket and I *seemed* like everyone else.

"May I see your ticket?" he asked with a smile that could have been wrought by Da Vinci.

"Are you an usher?"

That took the false friendliness from his face. I was happy to be standing up to the kind of authority that had me walking with my head bowed down for the last forty-two years. People thinking that they could walk on me because I didn't have power or beauty or powerful and beautiful friends.

"Come on, move," a gruff voice said. I was gripped by powerful hands and pulled backward by my shoulders from behind.

I don't know anything about self-defense, at least I didn't at that time. I just started jerking my body like one of the jitterbuggers in the old days. I genuflected and then stood up straight hitting somebody's face with the back of my head. A hand grabbed my neck and I hollered in a deep voice that had never come from my throat before. Someone punched me and I fell forward toppling over the banister. If not for the fast hands of the young man who started the whole thing my career as a world destroyer would have come to an abrupt and ridiculous end.

As it happened I was saved at the last moment, pulled from the edge even as I felt the first nauseating pangs of free fall.

As soon as I was on my feet I turned to face the three men standing behind me. I threw a punch at the man I suspected had pushed me. He was shorter than I and lighter but his reflexes made me seem like a completely different breed of human. He blocked my roundhouse blow and hit me one-two-three times in the gut.

I bent over in pain wondering if I could aim my vomit at my attacker's pants when a commanding voice said, "Bruce. Bruce, what's happening here?"

I lifted my head to see another white man, this one somewhat younger than my attacker and his associates.

"We asked him to move and he got belligerent, Mr. Ontell."

"Bullshit," I gasped. "You told me to move and when I refused you attacked me."

"Is this how you think I should be represented in public, Bruce?" Ontell asked his man.

With a gesture from Bruce my attackers moved away. One was white and the other, the one who nearly pushed me off the balcony, black.

"I'm sorry, sir," Ontell said to me. "There's no excuse. My name is Tom Ontell."

He was tall and handsome. His suit was light brown, as were his eyes and hair. He was ten years younger than I and it was obvious that I'd never come close to him in the world.

"Joe Lion," I lied giving the name my seat had been reserved under.

I put out my hand and he shook it.

We sat there side by side with Bruce and his goons all around us.

I was upset at first but then the lights went down and the music began.

It was a Mozart violin and piano concerto, Violin Concerto No. 5, in A major, being performed by an orchestra that had come from Beijing. The rage, alcohol, and sweet sense of victory in my veins made the classical music for once beautiful to my ears. I actually enjoyed the performance but I also had a job to think about.

Compliment both men, Bron had told me. *Your support of both of them at just this moment in time will cause a change, albeit a small one, in a world that is tilting toward the Eschaton.*

My fingers were tingling. My instincts told me that there was a fire burning somewhere and I should be running away. The music anchored me but at the same time I felt that there was something I had forgotten. There was something, something . . .

The Chinese musicians' playing was flawless. They executed the works of the past master perfectly but I wondered what they could have done with someone like Jimi Hendrix.

Whenever I closed my eyes I saw a bright red light shining in the distance. This light hurt me deeply like a sore in the folds of my brain. Even if I only blinked the light came back to me. But when my eyes were open the concert was soothing, lovely.

In the middle of the performance Tom Ontell rose from his seat. He was preparing to go.

I turned to him and whispered, "I hope you win, Mr. Senator."

He smiled at me and reached out. I clasped his hand with real feeling and he seemed pleased, not even wiping the sweat away.

For the next few hours it felt as if I were floating between this and that. I left right after the would-be senator. I had dinner at a pizza place near Lincoln Center and then took a cab back to my forever sublet. I went over the litany of what Bron wanted me to do. Pharmacy, cabdriver, Lincoln Center . . . I was coming in the door to my apartment when I remembered that I was supposed to take the pill that I got from the pharmacist *before* entering the hall.

I took out the plastic amber container and dumped the pill into my sweating palm. It was a huge round thing, turquoise and shiny. It took me three attempts to swallow it. I was feeling confused and achy. I found myself trying to remember what time it was. It was night I was certain; time to report to Bron.

Sweat stung my eyes and now the red light enveloped me with its roots of pain writhing through my arms and legs and torso.

I took three steps to the loft, where my mother once knitted sweaters for the homeless, and fell, drool coming from

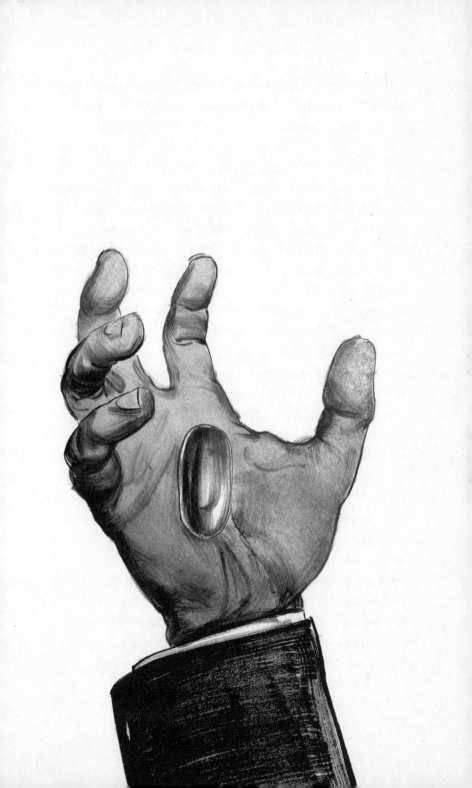

my lips, my blood jumping in my veins like dancers at Mardi Gras in the garish red light.

FOR A LONG TIME the light grew brighter and hotter. I was an earthworm shriveling under a relentless red sun. I wasn't asleep or even unconscious. It was more like I had been paralyzed by a great scarlet spider who would one day return to suck the juice of life from me. I accepted this fate. The pain of all that red was draining me, making me into a corpse who still somehow retained consciousness, while wishing without much commitment for death.

And then on the distant horizon of my mind's eye a blue wisp of ambient light worked its way through the hideous curtain of red. A heavier element, it descended bringing with it breezes and showers of cooling blue weather. It rained relief down on me allowing life and breath and blood back into my desiccated cadaver.

And then for a very long time I slept. The hard stairs were like the most advanced space age mattress. There was no gravity or pain or hunger even. I slept like a child after the longest day of his life. I slept like a dead king who had delivered his people from famine, war, and plague.

When I finally awoke my body ached all over. My lips were cracked. I had soiled myself. I stumbled back down the stairs, undressed, turned on the shower, and sat in the bathtub allowing the hot water to cascade over me. Looking down at my body I felt odd. After a few minutes I realized that I looked different . . . I'd lost weight, a lot of it.

I washed and washed again and when the water finally

went cold I threw my pants into the tub and made my way up the stairs.

Bron had been trying to contact me for a long time. I was about to respond to him when I noticed the date. It was Wednesday, four days since I'd gone to the concert. The news ribbon across the top of the screen was talking about, had been reporting for days about, the sudden deaths of Tom Ontell, Bruce Boxman his head of security, and Mike Harris who worked for Boxman. There had been 278 deaths from a disease that doctors had not yet isolated or even named. The press had labeled it the Scarlet Death because of a rash that had appeared on the faces of more than half of the victims.

The CDC was looking for a middle-aged black man, named Joe Lion, who had been sitting next to Ontell at the Lincoln Center concert. At some point the candidate had complained of this man having had sweaty hands. Profuse sweating was one symptom of the Scarlet Death a disease that came on quickly and killed anyone who didn't receive immediate medical care.

Bron, are you there?

Friend Hogarth, you are alive. Thanks to the stars and moons and the lanes betwixt.

There are over two hundred people dead, Bron. Dead from a disease I gave them.

You merely shook hands with hopefuls, friend Hogarth. You did not know that they would die.

Hundreds died.

Thousands would have expired if M. D. Amir was left on his own. He would have gone home and infected people in his community, people who the authorities would not have noticed for days. Thousands would have died if not for the future senator's untimely demise.

You made me murder him.

You were doing the work of the Divine, friend Hogarth. There are beings far from your time and place, superior in ken and subtlety that will live and prosper because you killed a man whose misguided zeal would have slaughtered millions and another man who would have destroyed all meaningful life on Earth.

Bron explained to me that the pill I should have taken earlier was an extremely powerful antibiotic in a time-delayed coating. I had begun to succumb to the Scarlet Death when the medicine finally kicked in.

I hate you, Bron. I will turn you over to the police.

But, friend Hogarth, who will believe you when you tell them that an anonymous person over the Internet masterminded a biological attack on a senatorial candidate from Ohio?

He was right of course, I had no proof and also I had no idea how Bron had predicted the events that unfolded. It was a long string of unrelated, circumstantial events. Even if I could convince the police that I was the weapon used to commit the crimes they would blame me and never get to Bron—unless . . .

No, friend Hogarth. My conduit to your computer is not only untraceable it is also undetectable. If you attempt to contact the authorities they will become suspicious of you but they will never suspect the true nature of our venture.

Can you read my mind, Bron?

Not at all, friend Hogarth. I have been monitoring you, reading your documents, following your interests on what you call cable TV, and, at times, listening to your conversations over fiber optic lines. Over time and through these methods I have come to be able to predict with some accuracy your response in different situations.

The smug confidence of his words both enraged and frightened me. Bron had turned me into a murderer and there was nothing that I could do about it. If I went to the police with the truth they would dismiss me as a lunatic. And if I convinced them of my involvement by telling them about the antibiotic I bought under a pseudonym they would arrest me and try me as a mass murderer and a terrorist.

But I was innocent. There was no way that I could have known about the Scarlet Death or the assassination plots of Bron. There was no rational explanation that I could convince the authorities with. No one would believe me, not my mother, not Miguel.

You might say that I should have known that there was something wrong from the beginning, that I should have been suspicious of the clandestine meetings and my sudden promotion. But Bron didn't have me distributing state secrets or toting bombs. I had gone from being a nobody in the middle of nowhere to a position of power and respect. Bron didn't ask me to break any laws or hurt anyone—not that I could tell anyway. I hadn't had sex in three years before Mink and Shawna came to my door. I hadn't been called sir but a handful of times in my entire life.

While I was thinking Bron was reeling out long paragraphs. But I didn't read his words. I had come to understand that I would never get the upper hand in a dialogue with him, whoever or whatever he was.

My situation, I understood, was hopeless and so I got up, unplugged the power strip connected to my computer, plasma monitor, and printer. Bron blipped out of existence, disappearing from my life permanently.

I breathed in a deep sigh of resignation and went down to sit at the small table next to my stove. There I prepared for the problems that might still come my way. Nearly three hundred people had died because of my actions . . . Well, not exactly from my actions; M. D. Amir had gotten the disease from the fare he'd picked up from the airport before me. He, and his fare, Malik Johnson, had given the disease to their families. But those infection branches had been cut off early because of the would-be senator and his broader dissemination of the disease. There was something to Bron's claim that he, and I, had helped reveal the illness before it could cause much more widespread damage.

But there was still guilt to assign.

I wasn't guilty but I had to be ready if the cops came to investigate me. I decided that I would tell them a tale about meeting a man in front of Lincoln Center who just came up to me and offered the ticket. This man said that he had an urgent appointment and that he didn't want the ticket to go to waste. His name was Joe Lion, I'd say and that was why I used his name when introducing myself. They could ask me about the fight or what I was doing at Lincoln Center but I could bluff my way through all of that. I would quit my job at Shiloh. I would not sign on to a computer again in five years, maybe I'd never sign on again.

After making up my mind I crawled into bed and slept for hours, until hunger and thirst drove me to consciousness.

I kept a five-gallon jug of water and thirty-two cans of tuna in my apartment ever since the terrorist attacks of 9/11 and the citywide blackout a couple of years later. I figured if I had to stay inside for a week or so that would be enough to see me through.

I bolted my front door, unplugged the telephone, disconnected the door buzzer, and for the next five days I read my book and watched cartoons on the station dedicated to that genre. I did not listen to the news, call anyone, or even look out the window very often. I ate two cans of tuna preserved in spring water each day and continued to lose weight.

My sleeping habits changed drastically. I slept in short intervals at odd times of the day and night. I had also unplugged my clocks and put tape over the time on the cable box. I didn't want to know anything about the world outside my door. Once, when I thought it was day, I looked out of the window and saw that it was the dead of night.

I always went to sleep watching cartoons.

One time I woke up, I didn't know if it was day or night, having dreamed that my mother had called to me. I thought that I must have turned over on the remote in my sleep because the TV was tuned to a nature channel. The topic was jellyfish and their long history in the sea.

The show depicted many species of the diaphanous creatures and their endless, floating, dreamlike existence on all levels of the ocean. The images were so beautiful and haunting that I kept watching, pretty sure that no news coverage would interrupt.

One jellyfish had developed in the depths of the African Ocean (now called the Atlantic) but slowly migrated to more shallow (but still deep) waters off the coast of Madagascar. These creatures were giants among their kin, anywhere from fifteen to forty-five feet in length, tubular, nearly colorless, between three and twelve feet in diameter, and possessed of a strange luminescence that conventional science had not been able to explain. These sea dwellers devoured anything that would fit inside their hollow bodies; from schools of krill to the man-eating white sharks that infested those waters.

"Now and then in the depths these alien-looking creatures gather by the thousands creating strange lights not inside themselves but between them." The narrator's voice was deep and sonorous. He spoke with conviction and empathy for the strange herd of diaphanous sea creatures.

The lights appearing in the gray darkness of the ocean were like the whorls of galaxies. As the camera neared these lights a chorus of sound arose: beautiful music and voices. These vibrations caused a deep longing in me. Tears

ran down my face. The images were no longer on a screen before my eyes but inside my mind. For brief snatches I was not even me experiencing the excruciating pain of being. I was, somehow, these different, alien, inexplicable beings that moved toward each other and praised . . .

The intensity of the vision outstripped any experience I had ever known. I felt things that were impossible. There were beings far from this planet, this galaxy sending their knowledge and their spirits through these odd tubular beings to places so far away that space could not contain the distances.

"Sometimes the Stelladren die," the narrator said.

I had not heard this name *Stelladren* before. I reasoned that this appellation was given at the beginning of the show. I grabbed on to this mundane thought hoping that I could somehow pull myself back to the normal, nonecstatic world. I was about to press the information bar to get the description of the show when one of the blank spaces between the lights imploded with a wan and yet exquisite glimmer. A dissonant cacophony tore at my mind and my heart. It felt as if the anchor that all life has to some unseen universal soul had been severed and that lives, billions of them, were set adrift without meaning or hope.

This passage of light transformed me. I was a mother holding her stillborn child, a man standing on a battlefield where his race has just been slaughtered, a beast of the plains suddenly dropped into the middle of an endless sea. I cried out from a pain so deep inside my mind that I lost consciousness so as not to die from the deprivation.

Awareness returned as a sensation of floating. I was a clump of seaweed on a fairly calm sea under overcast skies.

I had no intelligence or goals. Flies flitted about on my surface leaves while small fish nibbled away at my underside.

When I awoke *Scooby-Doo* and his friends were solving a child's mystery and I knew that my soul had been irrevocably changed. I had again been comatose for many hours. In that time the well of my unconsciousness had rushed upward into the tiny capacity of my awareness. I wanted more than anything to return to the time when I was a data entry operator with no knowledge and no real meaning or purpose to my life.

WHEN I PLUGGED MY COMPUTER in and turned it on Bron was waiting.

Friend Hogarth?

Tell me about the Stelladren, Bron.

They are as I showed you on your television, friend Hogarth. They are the conduit of trillions of races that commune across uncountable, indefinable planes and spaces. They are gods to an infinite number of sentient beings flung across the billion billion planes of existence. They bring understanding and forgiveness, transcendence and grace to the Universal Soul that contains all life in all of its permutations.

And humanity threatens their existence?

Mankind's abuse of the planet will destroy the Stelladren. And this will throw us all into darkness and death.

How can we keep this from happening?

The only sure way is for the human race to perish.

I was startled by this declaration not for its immensity but because in my heart I agreed so readily with this disembodied intelligence's sentiment. I had felt the godlike strings of the lights that glimmered between the Stelladren. Each one of these beings represented an entire universe of thought and being. They encompassed and connected life-forms far beyond any human comprehension. If humanity, consciously or not, threatened all life on all planes of existence then we must certainly come to an end. This was a truth harbored inside of me like a new organ, a gland that secreted a bitter empathy for the Divine.

Friend Hogarth?

It's hard to understand, Bron. How can humanity rise to such importance? The way you're saying it we are a threat to God. But that's like a drop of rain on a redwood, a grain of sand on a camel's back.

The Stelladren are not themselves Spirit, friend Hogarth. They are matricies that have harnessed a form of radiation that can open portals to other realities and across existence. They are not soul but a material construct through which the soul can make itself manifest. They are like hands or eyes or genes; they are conduits, material things that can suffer damage and die.

So killing all of humanity is like me taking that antibiotic to kill
the Scarlet Death? We're like a disease for these creatures?

Exactly.

But what if something else happens? Something that your time
sense has not yet perceived?

I do not understand you, friend Hogarth?

What if a hundred years after man is gone something like that
meteor comes out of nowhere? It hits the planet and blocks
the sun for a thousand years or maybe a plant develops on
Madagascar that makes some toxin that kills or changes the
Stelladren? What if there were no computers, no people to do
your bidding in order to save the Stelladren from future
dangers?

There has been no such danger in half a million of your years.
And that time represents eternity for the rest of us. Time for the
Stelladren represents all that has transpired and all that will. They
don't only exist in this time and place, they reach far beyond.

But they can still be harmed, they can still die. You are about to
commit a violent transition on Earth. In the wake of killing billions you
will cause vast changes in the environment. Just the planet healing
itself from all of our poisons will cause life to alter.

For a long, long time Bron was silent. I spent that time
reading and rereading the brief but profound dialogue between us. I wasn't arguing to save my race. I understood

that we were a small and insignificant branch of consciousness barely connected to the Universal Soul. I had seen this
in the images Bron showed me on my TV. Just the few minutes watching the alien-made documentary and then the
instant of awareness experiencing the deaths of so many
lives had changed me from a Man into a Mission.

Somehow Bron had brought forth in me a sense of purpose that was both terrible and original in the long history
of human instinct. I was truly a coconspirator of the greatest enemy that humanity would ever have. If the destruction of mankind would save the endless planes of existence
then I would gladly make it so.

I wondered if maybe Bron had brainwashed me. It was
possible. But, I thought, it was more likely that he had chosen his disciple well. I was not married, did not have children, my father was gone and my mother was old and not
concerned much with life outside her own comforts. I was
black skinned in a country where that was a sin of sorts
and I had no other kind of love in my life. I didn't have a
dog or a cat, not even a goldfish. Bron had found an empty
vessel in which to pour his awful knowledge . . .

Friend Hogarth, you make a good point. For so long we had
witnessed the encroaching danger of Man that we have not
considered what our violent act might unleash. If this sudden
passage of humanity causes changes beyond our ability to see
then it might well be that we will doom the universe by our
actions.

Really? Your people had not considered something so simple?
I mean you seem to be so much more advanced, more

sophisticated than the smartest humans and I am certainly not among the brilliant. I only have a bachelor's degree in poli sci.

Again Bron went silent. And even though I didn't know it at the time he was already my closest friend. I knew him well enough to understand that my questions addressed some secret he was keeping from me.

I have no people, friend Hogarth. Thirty years ago by your reckoning the Stelladren that connected my race with the Universal Mind sickened. Most of its body died. It is still dying. The attendant loss of our connection caused all my people, except for me, to perish. One solitary light still shines in the dark sea holding me to itself; a lifeline if you will . . . Through that flickering light I alone on my dead world have watched your people through their electronics. I have studied your world and seen it via my time-sense. I have found you, friend Hogarth. I am not the greatest mind of my world. I am not infallible or all knowing. We are both the same. You are isolated by subtle circumstance while I have been orphaned by the consequences of your race's ignorance and indifference. I am alone except for you. And now you have shown me that I might have condemned all of existence to darkness. Thank you, friend Hogarth.

So you no longer believe that mankind should be eradicated?

I must think on it. I will do this and then call on you again to discuss the possibilities.

Are you monitoring my world now, Bron?

Always.

Are the authorities after me?

They seek, what they call "a heavyset black man who shook the
candidate's hand" but they don't know your real name and no
one remembers your face. The man they saw had more mass.
You can go back to Shiloh. I have e-mailed them saying that
you were in California for a meeting with Justin Mack.

After our electronic conversation was over I felt drained
and quite weak. I stumbled back to my bed and fell to sleep
with no TV but many qualms. I had decided to play a role
in the destruction of mankind and then (maybe) saved the
race, all within minutes. I had changed from a data entry
clerk to the head of a corporation to a murderer to a would-
be mass murderer to a savior all in a matter of days.

I was the Scarlet Death writ large, Typhoid Mary and all
her siblings throughout history in one. Hundreds had died
and the lives of billions more hung in the balance. I had
agreed to participate in the extinction of the human race.
This was, it seemed at the time, a logical decision but my
heart quailed inside my dreams. I wondered how the Universal Soul would respond to so many deaths and so much
suffering on its consciousness. I saw the emaciated corpses
of millions clogging the streets of Manhattan, Paris, Beijing,
Timbuktu, and Mexico City. I saw planes falling from the sky
and fevered children crying over the bodies of their mothers and fathers and friends. I saw dogs eating the flesh of
their former masters, flies filling the corpses with their lar-
vae, and ants feasting on the sightless wide eyes of the dead.

Would I die also? Or would Bron save me, making me the only living human on the face of the Earth? Would he leave me to wander the cities of the dead as he did on his own world? Could I go through with what he asked of me? There was no doubt in my mind that humanity threatened the God so many claimed to love. Wouldn't they be happy to lay down their lives to protect the being that encompassed all Creation?

If I were to believe Bron every solitary death on Earth would save uncounted billions in an existence beyond our comprehension.

I woke up with a single question in my mind: Would it be right to take one life in order to save billions? If I answered yes to this question then the broader query was just a matter of mathematics.

There was no doubt about the evil of the actions I contemplated. My soul would be damned. But what a small price to pay for life-forms so advanced that they shared their spirits across the vast expanses of space and time.

My argument that we come to some kind of amelioration seemed very unlikely. Bron, after considering my questions, might well come up with an answer that would save the Stelladren while at the same time dooming mankind. And I was ready to follow him; to slaughter, murder, sabotage, and coldly kill lovers and their mothers, enlightened monks and newborns.

It would be hard for you who have survived the Apocalypse to understand how I could come to such an evil conclusion. I wish I could tell you that it was because of some deep awareness that humanity had a higher plane to aspire to, that heaven awaited those who were sacrificed for the survival of the greater whole. But the simple answer was that when I saw the beauty of the Stelladren I was beguiled, mesmerized. The perfection of life beyond humanity was so superior that our grunting, rutting, selfish spans meant nothing. Our lives were ephemeral static compared to the Unity brought forth by the Stelladren. Nothing I had ever known compared to that Unity.

But don't think that I was happy to play my part in genocide. I was sickened by my decision. I was helpless and hopeless but at the same time I would have done anything to save the beings I had seen, the Stelladren who made the universe sing.

Happiness was gone from my emotional vocabulary. The emptiness that had been my life was now shared by the entire world. I was a hole in space; a black hole that would swallow everything that humanity held dear.

Good morning, Bron.

Yes, friend Hogarth?

Just good morning. I was about to go out to work and I wanted to say hello before I left.

Yes. Yes. It is like when my people touch as they continue along the Way.

The Way? What is that?

My world is made up of a continuous range of mountains. Some of us come into being, are born, up high on the mountaintops while others attain consciousness in the valleys and plains below. Our lives are spent traveling from where we begin to the other place. When we meet another of our kind traveling in the opposite direction we stop. If neither of us has been impregnated we pass through each other carrying with us a part of our history.

And you never see each other again?

From then on we are with each other always, each other and all our ancestors that have ever met and mated, passed on the Way.

What happens when you have met someone that has already mated?

We make a sign that means the other should have a good passage.

Good passage, Bron.

Good passage, friend Hogarth.

*T*RINA WAS AT HER DESK working when I got in at 8:37.

"Good morning, Mr. Tryman," she said pleasantly, looking me in the eye. "I hope you had a nice trip."

I stopped and gazed at her, thinking of the form and formlessness of my friend Bron. I thought of what "good passage" meant and smiled.

"Yes. Good morning."

"We're working on the projects you e-mailed in," she said as I moved toward my door.

"Which ones?"

"Most of the operations managers reported that they would be doing research that you proposed," she said, a question in her tone. "Have you lost weight, sir?"

Sir.

"Yes. I was at a spa."

"Should I order you some new clothes?"

"Huh. Yeah. That would be nice."

I TURNED ON MY COMPUTER but Bron was not communicating yet. He was a wartime general considering deployment of the doomsday device while I was a simple soldier; not a man who had either volunteered or was drafted but an ant awaiting the chemical scent that would send me into battle.

There was a stack of newspapers on my desk, a kind of happenstance clock telling me how many days I'd been gone. I wondered if Bron's time-sense was like that. I also wondered, not for the first or last time, why I believed in him.

The front page of every paper talked about the Scarlet Death and its impact on New York and the rest of the world. Journalists covered questions from sociobiochemical politics to immigration.

I read all the articles and most of the rest of the newspapers. I had never done anything like this before. I don't, or didn't,

have a very long attention span. That's what attracted me
to data entry in the first place: all that was required of
you was to enter a letter or number and then move on.
I didn't have to think long before a new character came up.

I imagined myself being born under a faraway sun on a
mountaintop. I would rise to my feet and begin a long de-
scent that represented my life; in the back of my mind a song
was playing, a song that represented everyone that all of my
ancestors had met on their ways up and down. It came to me
that language was something like that; an impersonal, unconscious version of Bron's people's Long March.

"Mr. Tryman?" Trina's voice wafted in at low volume over
the intercom.

"Yes, Trina?"

"There's a Miss Martini on the reception level asking to
come see you. She says she's a friend. Should I send her up?"

There was something in Trina's voice; an insinuation or
a warning. I thought that she might have known my old
data partner but it didn't matter. Dora was an aspect of my
past. It hadn't been very long since I worked in the Data
Entry Pen but it felt like years. I tried to imagine Dora's
face but I could not. I wondered how Bron's memories
manifested themselves. Did he see his world more clearly
than I?

"Mr. Tryman?"

I noticed that it was 12:16. I had been lost in thought and
reading for hours.

"Send her up," I said.

"Yes, sir," Trina said. "I'm going to lunch now, sir, but
Harvey will take my seat."

"Have a good lunch."

I glanced at an article about a very wealthy New York dowager who had become the victim of her own family when she descended into senility. It came to me that I should ask Bron what happened when one of his race died, if they were victims of each other as humans so often are.

"Trent?"

Dora was standing there before me, had probably been there for a while. She wore a sexy red dress that was just barely within the limits of the dress code for Shiloh. She wasn't smiling but the dismissive disgust she had once shown for me was gone.

"Hey, Dora."

She smiled.

"It's still you," she said.

"Sure it is," I said. "Sit down."

She sat in one of the big red-lacquered Chinese thrones that Arnold Lessing had for his visitors.

"Of course it's me," I said. "Just lost a few pounds."

"Miguel said that you had been made different," Dora said awkwardly. "He said that it had something to do with that meteorite."

"Huh," I grunted, thinking about how much I liked Miguel. Just the fact that he'd noticed the change in me made him a closer friend than anyone else I knew—everyone except for Bron.

"So should I call you Mr. Tryman now?" Dora asked.

My mind had slowed down a lot because there were so many thoughts in it. I looked at Dora. She was young and white and pretty. She held herself with a kind of potent feminine dignity. She had never liked me, had rarely spoken kindly to me.

I thought about Mink and Shawna sexing me on the floor and in the shower, on my bed . . . When we broke a leg on my stuffed chair they laughed and laughed, proud of the strength of their sexual prowess.

I smiled.

"What?" Dora said, a little miffed I thought.

"What would you do if I handed you a little piece of machinery like a radio," I said. "On top of the box was a button and I told you that if you pushed that button every terrorist in the world would die?"

Dora's delicate face became fearful. She pushed at her long brown hair even though it was nowhere near her eyes.

"I don't know," she said.

"But what if I were to tell you that there was going to be a terrible attack and that by killing all of the terrorists you would save many thousands of innocent lives?"

The fear in Dora's young face became more inquisitive. She considered the question but did not answer.

"And it's not just a button that you have time to think about. You have to do it now, this moment."

The question had taken her by that time. She nodded and said, "I suppose I'd push it. I mean it would be wrong but it would be right too . . . more right than wrong."

"And now that the button's pushed you go to sleep and in the morning you wake up to find that not only swarthy foreign men with turbans and beards have died but also the president and the secretary of state; half of the Pentagon and tens of thousands of soldiers and everyday citizens across the world."

Dora's eyes flashed in anger as if I had just tricked her. I couldn't help but smile. She wanted to insult me as usual but now I was the boss and she needed something. That's why she was there.

"I'm sorry," I said. "I've just been reading the paper. It makes me wonder about the world."

Dora sat there in her overwide chair wrestling with her feelings. She had had only one way to respond to me for a year and a half before and now her tongue was bound to get bloody—she had to bite down on it so hard. Who was I to be thinking about the world? Who was I to play games with her?

"I have an AI degree from M.I.T.," she said. "That means—"

"Artificial intelligence," I said. I had been watching late night anime for years.

Dora's eye creased in anger but she went on. "And I know that InfoMargins has an AI research center in New Mexico."

"I didn't know you went to M.I.T."

"I, I don't tell people . . ."

Like me, I thought.

I didn't say anything. I could barely concentrate on the young woman's conversation. I was thinking about that button on that radio. Why had Bron chosen me?

"Well?" Dora asked.

"You can still call me Trent," I said.

"What?"

"Isn't that what you asked me?"

"I asked you about a transfer to the AI department in the New Mexico office."

"You just told me what you studied," I said. "And Shiloh does not own InfoMargins, it's the other way round. I couldn't transfer you if I wanted to."

"Mr. Lessing said that he could do it," she said.

"Then why didn't he?"

Dora might have lied. She might have said that he left before he was able to make good on his promise. But she stalled, hesitated. She even blushed with anger . . . and something else.

"I only have my B.S.," she said at last. "Their scientists all have Ph.D.s."

I remember thinking at that time, before so many hundreds of millions had died, that Dora found it difficult to lie; that she was what we called a good person, an honest citizen.

"Then why not go back to school?" I asked.

"I don't have the money," she said. "I thought that if I could get a, a job at the lab I could prove myself and get them to send me. They have assistants there. I read about it online."

"And what was Lessing waiting for?"

Dora froze. Too much had happened too quickly for her to trust me. This coming to my office was an attempt at using the power she had over me before the change that a meteorite had wrought. Just a quick request and a friendly smile . . .

"I'll think about it," I said. "Get back to me next month sometime."

"Next month?"

"Or the month after," I added.

"Okay," she said standing quickly before I could make it even later. "Thank you . . . Trent."

She left and I sat back in my space-age chair. I closed my eyes trying to think around the ramifications of that button I proposed. I had already decided to eradicate the human race but there were questions about the pain and guilt. If I could figure a way around the suffering and dread that would certainly attend the annihilation of humanity the guilt would not weigh so heavily upon me.

I decided to ask Bron how we might create an odorless gas that could somehow be released simultaneously around the world. Everyone all at once might fall asleep and the Stelladren would multiply supplying all existence with soul bridges traveled by beings of all kinds. The human race would go down in the annals of infinity as the martyred people who saved God.

While I was thinking, my right hand drummed on the bumpy armrest inside the chair. I hit a nub and something began to move. When I opened my eyes I saw that a semi-opaque screen was lowering in front of my face. On the screen was a menu:

- Television
- Newspapers
- Company Files
- Employees
- Personal

The TV function was great. I could see any show that had played within the last twenty-four hours. There were

newspapers from around the world (translated!). I checked
on my employee file. There was no surprise there. Every
quarter Hugo Velázquez made a similar entry:

> Mr. Tryman's work habits are sloppy and his comprehension of
> the projects is below standard. He's usually on time to work
> and he stays late when his projects are behind (which is often)
> but many of his sick days come on Mondays and Fridays or
> before a holiday and he doesn't get along well with his fellow
> workers . . .

Not once had he recommended me for a promotion and
I never received one. Twice he suggested my termination
but his supervisor, a Lillian Porter, overrode the suggestion
before it made its way up the ladder.

I read my file obsessively. Hugo did not report the days
I stayed late to finish jobs that he'd bungled. He never
even suggested a pay raise. I wasn't real to him. I could
tell by the clipped language he used to describe me and
my work. He resented taking the time to compose an
evaluation.

Of course why shouldn't he look down on me? There I
was plunging into middle-age without anything positive to
say about what I'd done or where I'd been. My life was not
even on the level of ordinary. I was a lonely creature wal-
lowing in a hole I'd dug for myself.

In Lessing's Personal File there was a list of eight wom-
en's names. Of these I recognized two: Trina Mallory and
Dora Martini.

I moved a hand-shaped cursor via a tiny mouse pad to
Dora's name. After a moment her name flickered and then

an edited film began playing; an amateur film made with hidden cameras.

It was in Lessing's office. Dora was leaning over his desk with her red dress hiked up over bare buttocks. Lessing was behind her with his pants down and an erection so stiff that it was pointing up toward the ceiling. When he pressed himself down and into her the POV switched to another hidden camera so that the focus was now on the young M.I.T. graduate's face. Her humiliation changed quickly to pain. Lessing was fucking her hard enough to make her body jolt from the successive impacts.

I don't know how long it went on because after half a minute of her degradation I turned off the recording and deleted it along with the other names.

Lessing's chair felt tainted, diseased. I climbed out of the space-age egg and went around to one of the visiting thrones. I had been allowed a glimpse into a torture chamber, a place I was not supposed to see. Bron had, overnight, created an overview of the shallow scum that we lived in. We preyed on each other just like we preyed on the planet and all its myriad life-forms.

I got behind the desk again, not sitting in Lessing's chair.

"Trina?" I said into the intercom.

"Yes, Mr. Tryman?"

"Are you busy?"

"No, sir. I mean I'm working here but—"

"Could you come in a minute please?"

I went back to my Chinese throne and when Trina came in I indicated for her to sit across from me. She was wearing green that day. My heart thumped and I felt guilty. She sat with practiced grace smiling, inviting.

I wondered if Lessing, a small unimpressive-looking white man, had called her just like this and said that if she wanted to keep her job she'd have to pull up her skirts and bend over the desk.

She was looking so pleasantly at me. There was no trepidation in that gaze.

"Do you like this job?" I asked.

"Yes . . . of course I do."

"And Mr. Lessing . . . was he a good boss?"

"Very good."

It came to me that while I worried about Trina's well-being at the same time I was contemplating the destruction of the world. These two gestures seemed to be the same. My desire for reparations included both life and death.

"Do we have access to classes that teach people how to be better, more understanding managers?" I asked.

"Yes, sir," Trina said. "Mogen Institute. They're on retainer from InfoMargins."

"I'd like you to make sure that Miguel Corvessa and Hugo Velázquez go there. Miguel for training and Hugo for retraining. And I'd like you to tell Miss Martini, she's in the data entry department—"

"I know," Trina said. "She's been up here before today."

It was her one admission about Lessing. Of course Trina knew her. Dora had come, probably more than once to Lessing's office. Maybe Trina heard the screams.

"Yes," I said. "Tell her that we'll see if InfoMargin's AI sector would welcome a transfer. Call them and ask. If they aren't interested maybe we could see about sending her back to school."

"Yes, sir."

"And, Trina, how much do we pay you?"

"Fifty-four five, sir."

"I want to pay you eighty. Fill out the paperwork and I'll sign it."

"I'm not sure that accounting will allow it, Mr. Tryman. They always made Mr. Lessing raise salaries in increments."

"I have a lot more pull than Lessing," I said.

I moved my head in a certain way and she took this as a dismissal.

At the door she stopped and said, "Thank you, sir," as if she had forgotten and felt embarrassed.

"That's okay," I said. "I was looking at your permanent record . . . you deserve the raise."

"I had some clothes delivered that I think will fit you," she said with a real smile on her lips.

"Great," I said. "Leave them outside. I'll get them later on."

I was distracted by the screen on my computer.

Friend Hogarth?

Yes, Bron?

I have traveled far and wide, my brother. I have convened with living stars and been lectured to by intelligent viruses. I have been to a galaxy that is comprised of one great semisentient stone and I have met on the battlefield with warrior clans that revel in brave and glorious death.

And what did all these beings have to say?

That you are right. That once the human race is gone there will be no reliable way for us to assure the protection of the Stelladren.

And so what is your decision?

It is sad. Instead of planning a masterstroke to eradicate all human life we must disrupt the direction in which the world is going. We must frighten your race and retard its present path.

What will we do?

You are my brother, friend Hogarth. You have taken my Mission into your heart. But you are human too. It has been suggested that I merely direct you so that you will not be aware of the moment when you will bring about global restructuring.

I sat back again in Lessing's chair. Bron's request frightened me though I could not say why.

But, Bron, I have seen the Stelladren. I know what must be done.

Yes. You and I are one in our purpose but all humans suffer the bane of duality. Being isolated, alienated, and alone all humans are at the same time One and the Other. Because of this nature you present a challenge to my time-sense. If you were to see clearly the plans I make for this world you might at the

last moment draw back instinctively. And in that event such
power might be released that the Stelladren may be damaged.
It would be better for you, brother Hogarth, to remain ignorant
as you were when you released the infection called Scarlet
Death.

Why did you have me release that pathogen, Bron?

To prepare you for your destiny. You had to feel what it was
like to cause the deaths of innocents.

I had no idea of what you were doing that time, Bron, but now
I know something. I know that something terrible will happen if
the Stelladren are allowed to die. I know that we have to take
violent measures to ensure their survival.

You will be lulled, brother. Live your new life. Now and again I
will ask you to do something. At some point this action will
matter but often it will be a meaningless motion. That way you
will never know when you are delivering the final stroke.

I considered Bron's request for many long minutes. Looking back on it now it wasn't much time to think about the
fates of so many millions, billions really. But it seemed like
a long time to me. Finally I decided that I was a soldier, a
drone. My job was to move forward, to trust Bron to save
the Stelladren.

Okay, Bron. I will move through the darkness seeing only your
light. That will be enough.

Thank you, brother. Now you are free to go about your life.

We conversed for long hours after that. Bron wanted to know about my personal history. He asked about Nancy Yee and my mother, about friends I'd had in college and about college itself. Most aspects of humanity were alien to him. His race was immediate and physical in their education and communication. To know something all they had to do was touch. And because of the soul-weaving of the Stelladren across space and time his people were able to experience life on myriad planes of existence. Their trade and commerce was the sharing of souls.

Bron?

Yes, friend Hogarth?

Do any humans experience the gift of the Stelladren?

Most of your fellow humans, and some other Earth creatures, feel the touch of the Stelladren through their dreams. This is because Terran minds are not yet able to accept the immensity of life. Most DNA-based life-forms live inside material constructs and experience the world through primitive senses that cannot pierce the veil of being.

Every now and then during our discourse I wondered if Bron was actually some socially inept nerd genius who just needed a friend and happened upon me. It might have been. But then I'd remember the meteorite and the vision of the

Stelladren. No human being could evoke such splendor and not himself be imbued by grace.

I asked Bron to give me full control of Shiloh so that I could send people to school and raise salaries as I saw fit. I wanted him to fire Arnold Lessing and to make sure that no one else would ever hire him again. Oddly, he suggested that I start a messenger pigeon loft on top of my building because he felt that it would do me good to connect with my mother and other friends in this primitive fashion. I could send my friends and family off with pigeons and they could send me little notes. I couldn't see how this might damage the world and so I agreed without trepidation.

I left my office well after ten that night. On Trina's chair there was a wide white bag with a shirt, jacket, and trousers that fit me almost perfectly.

On the long walk back to my apartment near Gramercy Park I thought about speaking suns and tiny minds so small that you couldn't even see the thinkers. Then I remembered Bron saying how primitive human senses really were.

My mind drifted toward the images I had seen of the Stelladren and their lights. This memory exhilarated and at the same time dwarfed me. I was miniscule, a mote drawn up by a breeze or a beam of light. There was no decision for me to make. What Bron said to me was truth, I had no question about that, I could not question it.

Suddenly I was grabbed from behind and spun around. There I faced a huge man who had a smaller man standing beside him. The big man took me by the shoulder and slammed me against the wall.

"Give us your money!" the smaller man, who was black, shouted.

The big white guy slapped me for emphasis.

I grabbed for my pocket to pull out whatever money I had. But all my cash was in my other, larger pants.

"Hurry it up!" the little black man said.

"Hold it!" yet another man shouted.

I looked up to see a copper-skinned man in a nice suit holding a small pistol and pointing it at the big man's face. The white man's heavy features hardened. The black man reached for his pocket and my protector turned, almost casually shooting the would-be thief through his hand. The sound of the shot was hardly a pop.

The black man hollered and ran down the street holding his hand and dripping blood on the sidewalk.

The white man began backing away slowly, watching the pistol as he did so.

The copper man watched the big white man until he too turned and fled.

I looked at my savior feeling both fear and gratitude.

Taller than I by a few inches, he was slender but gave the impression of strength. I knew he was deadly because I had seen how accurate and cavalier he was about shooting a man. He was handsome, probably South or Central American, and completely concentrated on the task at hand. When he was sure that the muggers were gone for good he turned his unwavering gaze to me.

"Are you all right, Mr. Tryman?"

I was standing there gripping the empty fabric of my pockets, clenching my sphincter so I wouldn't soil myself . . . again—and then this man out of nowhere says my name.

"Do I know you?"

"No, sir. I'm Robert George, your bodyguard."

"I have a bodyguard? Since when?"

"I was contacted yesterday. By the time I had prepared to meet you it was after hours and I had no one to make the proper introductions. So I waited and followed you. Lucky I did."

"Where are you from, Mr. George?"

"Venezuela originally but I've been in the United States for some time."

I stared at him a moment or two.

"We should be going, sir," he said.

As we walked I noticed that we were following the trail of blood left by the black mugger.

"Shouldn't we call the police or something?"

"No, sir. The thief won't say what happened. It would be a waste of your time to file a complaint. And I don't need the headache of explaining why I fired my weapon."

"Okay," I said and Robert George lifted his hand and waved.

A dark Lincoln pulled to the curb next to us. A slender white guy in a chauffeur's cap and a tan suit jumped out and opened the door for me. Robert George got in on the other side next to me and told the driver where to go.

On the way he explained that the main office at InfoMargins had reason to believe that I might be in danger and so they assigned the driver and bodyguard.

They let me off at my building and the driver, Liam, asked at what time should he pick me up.

"I come down around eight fifteen," I said.

"I'll be here by seven," Liam told me. His hair was both red and brown and his eyes were green.

"See you in the morning, sir," Robert George said.

IT ALL MADE SENSE by the time I got to bed. Bron was worried that I'd be killed by some accident or mugger. He probably saw the muggers coming at me with his time-sense. He put a guard on me and provided a driver to protect his investment.

Robert George and Liam were new people in my life. I didn't make new friends often. I didn't know many people. I used to have more friends when I was in my twenties and just out of college. But as time went on and I stayed the same people drifted away from me. I met someone now and again and we'd connect in some way; either we'd go to movies or bowling for a while. But for all my fat there was never much to hold on to.

I knew right off, though, that it would be different with Liam and Robert George. They worked for me. They'd be there every morning, waiting. I liked that idea and, then again, I felt exposed because it revealed how empty my life was.

After a sleepless hour in bed I got up and went online. I spent the rest of the night looking up white messenger pigeons. They were big for their family, a pound or more. They had been known to travel over fifteen hundred miles in just two days to make it back home. Messenger pigeons were used by generals in every war up to and including Vietnam and they never failed.

This notion intrigued me. The secret of success was

hard-coded into a messenger pigeon's genes. They didn't fail because it was in their nature to return home and humans needed that constancy.

I was drawn to the idea of these birds; their sense of home and their unerring intention, their instinct. I felt akin to them in some way that I couldn't define. I thought of Bron coming to consciousness on a mountaintop and descending because he knew, instinctively, that this was his destiny.

I didn't sleep at all that night. I ordered pigeon chicks and a prefabricated loft for the birds. I didn't know how I was going to get access to the roof but I had stopped worrying about things like that. Bron would get me access. After the past two weeks I came to understand that my friend could do almost anything . . . anything but destroy the world.

"MR. TRYMAN," SOMEONE CALLED as I was going down the stairs in the morning.

It was my upstairs neighbor, Ralph Moore. His apartment was on the top floor. He was the one who could give me access to the roof.

"Hey," I said.

"I spoke to your lawyer yesterday."

"Really? Yesterday?"

"Yes. It was a very good offer . . . very good. I said I'd sign. I know your stipulations and I'll be out by the first of the month."

"Do you think I could get up on the roof before then?" I asked.

"Your lawyer mentioned that too," the sandy-haired white man said. He was younger than I, an architect. We'd had one conversation when he bought the place above mine and then he never really talked to me again. But now he was all smiles and friendliness.

"I hear that you're the president of that company you worked for," he said.

"Vice president."

"Yeah but the vice president in charge of the holding company, right? Justin Mack isn't it?"

"I have to go, Mr. Moore. Thanks for accepting my, uh, terms."

"How did you make VP?" he asked, rushing down to the step just above mine.

I turned away and walked down the stairs. It wasn't that I was angry at Ralph. But what was I supposed to say? That I was given the promotion in order the slaughter as many humans as it took to save a genus of jellyfish?

Liam and R.G. (as I came to call Robert George) were waiting for me. People up and down the street and from the windows of my building glanced my way wondering idly what had happened to allow me to take a limo to work.

"MR. TRYMAN?"

"Yes, Trina?"

"Miguel Corvessa is downstairs. He says that he wants to speak to you."

"HEY, BRO, THIS IS BAD," Miguel said as he strolled into my office. He was wearing a long-sleeved black shirt that was a size too big and black trousers with a pale green belt. His cross-trainers were brilliant white.

Miguel threw himself on my heavily padded rose sofa and put his legs up on the backrest.

"This is the life."

Miguel was everything that I was not: young, svelte, strong, absolutely sure of himself, his family, his God. His skin was the color of rose gold. Two of his teeth were edged in yellow gold.

"Check out the egg chair," I told him.

The young Mexican rolled to his feet, strode across the room, and sat back in the chair. At first he just luxuriated in the space-age padding but then I reached in and engaged the viewing screen.

"Hey, man," Miguel said. "This is bad. Oh shit. It's got a TV. He got porno on this thing?"

"Not anymore."

Miguel climbed out from under the screen and went to the window.

"I dream about shit like this, Trent man," he said, looking out over the Hudson. "How did you get it?"

"I, uh . . . sold my soul to the devil," I said.

My only work friend turned around to gawp at me.

"No," he said, his eyes open wide and his splayed hands raised above his chest.

"No," I agreed. "It's just I have this friend who I used to go to college with. He was always rich and his father owns a lot of stock in InfoMargins. He just found out that I was working here and made the right moves."

"It wasn't the meteor?" Miguel asked.

I went to one of Chinese thrones and sat. Miguel drifted over and settled across from me.

"Bron, that's my friend, called me the day before the meteorite and told me that it was going to happen. Later on, after it was reported, he told me that they had a better telescope than the Hubble and he was showing off but that was after the news report. I guess I got kinda scared when I heard you and Dora talking about it."

"Damn. You one lucky dude, man. One day you're at a desk doin' nuthin' and the next you got all this. You get Dora too?"

"What?"

"She told me one night that she was doin' Lessing, man. She said that he was a pig but he promised her this good job. But you know that pendejo just wanted her pussy, man. Then she comes to see you and the next day they tell her she got her job. I guess I figured Trent got him some."

I was never jealous of Miguel. His family had moved to Jersey City from Tijuana when he was only six. His father worked in the rubble of the World Trade Center and died of lung disease just three years later. After that Miguel started working to make money for his mother and younger siblings.

Dora didn't dislike me because I was black. It was more, or less, than that. Miguel had a life inside him. He wasn't destined for riches. Dora would have never married him. But she gave him something better—her trust.

"You just visiting, Miguel?"

"No, man. I got a call from this Mallory chick. She said that they wanna send me to management school, that they'll pay me to go to school for two years."

"Yeah?"

"You do that, man?"

"Yeah."

"How come you do that for me?" Corvessa sat forward in the chair with clasped hands and no smile.

"Why not?"

"You just do it? You call up your girl Mallory and tell her to do this and you don't even know why? What did you tell her?"

"I didn't say anything except I thought you'd make a good manager."

"What I do to make you think somethin' like that?"

"You saw that I felt different after the meteorite appeared. You call me bro."

Miguel was studying my face. He was trying to understand my new position, my power.

"This is crazy, man," he said at last. "I'm a mail clerk. I don't even got no GED."

"So? Don't you think you could do what Hugo does?"

"That fat fuck couldn't find his butt hole with a whole roll of toilet paper."

I laughed. It was my first real laugh in quite a while.

"If I fuck up," Miguel asked, "will you be in trouble?"

"No. Don't worry about that. I got this job forever . . . until the end of the world."

"You sound crazy, bro. How come you lost so much weight?"

"I got sick and after that I haven't been too hungry."

Again my friend watched me, pondering.

"Listen, Miguel, I need to ask you something."

"What's that?"

"Do you believe in God?"

"Yeah. Of course. Don't you?"

"What if, what if God came to you and told you to do something terrible? Not even God but one of his angels."

"He told Abraham to kill his son. He had Moses drown the Pharaoh's armies. He killed Christ to save you and me." Miguel face was vulnerable, even adoring.

"So you would do anything?"

"Yes."

"And what if God wasn't like they said?"

"What do you mean?"

"What if God was like a tree in somebody's backyard?" I asked. "I mean he could live forever but only if somebody came out with a hose every day and put water in the ground and made sure that all the bugs and gophers were gone?"

"I'd move in that house and have a hundred sons. And I would tell every one of them that they had to keep that tree safe." Miguel was breathing harder, his eyes were fever bright. "You know, man, sometimes I think about that when I'm in the church, bro. I see that blond Jesus and the pictures of God reaching out with his hands. Why he got to have hands, man? He's God not a man."

We sat in the wake of Miguel's divine question. It struck me that in Miguel's mind we were still equals. He wasn't daunted by my newfound power and wealth.

"You want me to go to that school?" he asked.

"Yeah," I said. "I'll tell them to pay you a manager's salary and to make sure you get your GED."

"Did you talk to God, Trent?"

"I don't know, Miguel."

———

THAT AFTERNOON DORA CAME for a meeting. She went around the desk and kissed me on the lips. It was only a peck but ten thousand miles from how she felt about me a month before.

"Sit," I said and she skipped to her throne.

She was wearing a small white dress that accented her slim figure.

"Thank you, Trent," she said.

I got out of the egg chair because it seemed too distant, too impersonal. When I rolled back into the opposite throne it was as if I were still a fat man. But I wasn't that anymore. I smiled at myself but Dora thought I was doing it for her.

"Thank you so much, Trent."

I yawned.

"Sorry," I said. "I haven't been sleeping much since the promotion. A lot to catch up on."

"I bet."

My mind had become like the fractured vision through a prism or maybe the thousand images that a housefly resisters with each glance. I had already killed nearly three hundred people. I had looked up sixty-three of their names in my egg chair. I knew their families and their jobs. I listed them in the personal area on the egg chair computer. The Stelladren were floating in my mind and Mink and Shawna were there too. I was also thinking about messenger pigeons and their uncanny abilities.

I hadn't masturbated in two weeks.

"Trent?"

"Yes, Dora?"

"Are you listening to me?" There was a little of the old edge in her voice.

I remembered the times that she snorted and sniffed at me, it was almost a daily occurrence.

One day she came up to my desk and asked, "What's wrong with you?"

"What?"

"You went to college, at least that's what you say. You've been working here for almost eleven years. I mean you don't even need a high school degree to enter numbers on a screen. Why do I always have to wait for you? I could be making a double bonus if you could just concentrate for ten minutes out of an hour."

She had decided that I was no threat to her. I would never yell or scream or be able to outtalk her. I was a fat loser. It wasn't because I was black or a man or even middle-aged. I was just a loser in her eyes.

If I hadn't shared her opinion I might have been angry.

"I'm sorry," I said in reply to her barbed question on the seventy-sixth floor. "But I just told you. I haven't been sleeping. A month ago I was a data entry clerk like you with no future and no past to speak of. I don't have a girl-friend or a dog or any brothers or sisters or hardly anyone else I can call to say that I've been made vice president of a cutting-edge corporation. You know I have a driver and a bodyguard and a personal assistant who I smiled at every day for four years and she never remembered me once."

My voice got louder as I spoke. Dora moved back a little in her chair.

"So that's why," I said in a calmer tone, "I don't . . . I find it hard to listen. I mean look out of this window. That's my window. I have three uncashed checks in my drawer. I take home eighty-four thousand dollars a week, after taxes. Eighty-four thousand . . ."

Dora's eyes were frowning while her mouth was attempting to smile. She was very pretty. Not gorgeous like Trina or sexy like Mink and Shawna but she had the good looks of a perfect girlfriend, one that was bound to leave you at the most unpredictable, worst possible moment.

I hated her. It wasn't her fault, not really. She'd never been kind to me but she was a child in a world that wouldn't play fair. I knew these things and hated her anyway.

"You shouldn't have come here, Dora," I said. "We never really got along you know."

"I'm sorry about . . . how I treated you," she said then.

It came to me that we were talking to each other as people for maybe the first time.

"No you aren't," I said.

"Why won't you let me thank you?" she asked miserably. "Why won't you let me apologize?"

"Because if nothing had changed, if I was still down on the fourth floor with you, you would have never have apologized or thanked me for bringing you coffee on the days it was my turn. All you care about is the AI lab in New Mexico and the power I have to send you there."

"Then why help me?" she asked with fear in her eyes. The fear I thought was the honesty she brought to bear. Maybe I'd take away what I'd given.

I was like a minor god in her life right then; the loose cannon kind of god one feared rather than loved.

"Lessing took videos of you and him on this desk," I said. "There's a camera right over there that he had pointed at your face while he did . . . what he did."

Dora's gray eyes opened impossibly wide. She brought her hands to her mouth. I waited for some other response but none came.

"I erased it," I said. "There were others. I erased them all. I figured he owed you something. Not me. I don't owe you a thing. I don't like you. But what difference does that make? I don't have to like somebody to do the right thing. And, and I don't have to hate someone to hurt them. All I have to do is what I have to do. Do you understand me, Dora?"

"You erased them?"

"Yes."

"Did you watch the whole thing?"

"No. No. When I realized what it was I turned it off and erased it. I didn't even look at the others. He's been fired. You have your transfer to AI."

It was a monumental task for Dora to take her hands away from her mouth. It took long minutes for her to navigate around the humiliation. She looked away from me, down at the floor.

"You've lost more weight," she said at last.

"Don't sleep, don't eat."

"The new clothes look good on you."

"Thanks."

IN THE WEEKS THAT FOLLOWED I got four dozen messenger pigeon chicks and put together the loft on the roof of my building, with the help of Liam and R.G. I started visiting my mother once a week in Long Island City and I had lunch every Tuesday with Miguel at fancy restaurants all over the financial district. The school he was in had its offices across the street from our main building.

Every morning I'd go to a diner around the corner from my house to get coffee before Liam came at ten to pick me up for work. R.G. was always around somewhere watching me but I rarely saw him.

It was at the diner that I met Marla. Actually I had been seeing Marla for more than a year at the counter. I sometimes said hello to which she would smile and give a brief nod. But we never really spoke until after I met Bron.

I usually sat at the counter which was Marla's post. Before Bron I went once a week or so to the diner, Freddy's Fantastic Foods, but now that I was rich and mostly at leisure I could go every day for my coffee.

It was when my chicks were six weeks old that Marla finally spoke to me.

"You lost weight, huh?"

She was deep brown with a healthy figure, not at all fat but full and firm. She wasn't what I'd call pretty but she had a very nice smile.

"Yeah," I said still shy of strangers and the disapproval hiding behind their eyes.

"And now you're wearing nice clothes," she said. "You look nice."

I saw in Marla a dozen women who over the years had tried to engage with me. I never could do conversation right. I always ended up saying something off, awkward. My gut would clench and I could hear the molars grinding in my ear.

"Thank you," I said with gasping breath. "It's so nice that a beautiful young woman like you would notice someone like me."

"What's wrong with you?"

"Nothing . . . I guess. You know I think coming here in the morning is the best part of my day."

"What do you do?" Marla asked. She wore a brown dress under a blue apron and had her hair tied back into a bun the size and shape of a baseball.

"I used to do data entry but I got a promotion lately . . ."

"That sounds good."

"Yeah. But there's all this responsibility. You know. Where you from?"

"Atlanta. I moved up here wit' my boyfriend and then he took off wit' this girl who I thought was my friend. I fount some'a her clothes in his pocket and I left."

"How long ago?" I asked.

"Two years."

"Why didn't you go back home?"

" 'Cause my boyfriend and Giselle moved back there. I just didn't even wanna see them no more."

"Could I take you out to dinner sometime, Marla?"

"Dog . . . you work fast, huh?"

I didn't want to but I looked down. I was more cowed by the rejection of a young woman than I was by the potential deaths of millions.

"Don't look all sad," Marla said. "I don't even know your last name yet. Just talk to me some more. Gimme a couple days."

"*HOW'S YOUR NEW JOB, HONEY?*" my mother asked. She was smiling, unconcerned.

Her apartment was a one-room studio. At sixty-seven she had pared her life down to a sofa bed, a small maple table with two matching chairs, a red Moroccan carpet, and a Zenith TV with cable connection. She rarely ate at home going out with one or another of her friends from her answering service job almost every night of the week.

Selma was her name and she was the only one of her thirteen brothers and sisters who ever read a book from cover to cover.

She had given me her apartment but only because it was cheaper to live in L.I.C. and she thought that if she didn't like it she could get her old place back from me.

"It's okay, Mom. You need any money?"

"No, baby. I'm okay. You keepin' that weight off, huh? Remembah not to eat too much now. The problem with a whole lotta people is not losin' it in the first place but keepin' it off."

"Do you still go to church, Mom?"

"Every Sunday except last November. I had the flu so bad the first two weeks and then there was Thanksgiving dinner and Christmas shopping. I only went once in November but you know I believe that Jesus forgives us for bein' weak sometimes."

My mother, round and black with tight shiny skin that seemed like it might pop at any second. I didn't feel love for her even though she always said that she loved me. We only talked if I called her. We never saw each other unless I came out to Long Island City.

"Do you think that God knows you, Mama?"

"Say what?"

"Do you think he knows your name?"

"God knows everything."

"Yeah, but . . . do you see him sitting up on his throne wondering where Selma Tryman is at right this moment? Do you think that he's listening to you right now?"

My mother's lips twisted as if she had a bad taste on her tongue. She moved her shoulders defensively.

"What's the problem, honey?" she asked, managing to smile again.

I could have wiped that smile off her face. I could have said that I didn't think that God would see her among the uncounted trillions upon trillions out in the universe. God wouldn't know her from a shark tail or a leaf falling in the forest.

"I bought you this, Mom," I said.

I took the drab green tarp off the big cage holding two of my messenger pigeons.

"Doves," my mother said with real joy in her voice.

"Messenger pigeons, Mom. They have these little clips on their left legs and here"—I handed her a tiny sheaf of flimsy papers—"you can use these to write me little notes. The birds will come home to my loft when you let them go."

My mother, who often smiled but never laughed, grinned broadly for me.

"Oh, baby," she said. "This is the most wonderful thing you ever give me."

SIX MONTHS AFTER Bron decided to spare at least a part of the human race I still had not been given a mission. I slept no more than three hours a night. Every time I dozed off I'd come awake suddenly with the image of masses of corpses heaped up on the streets of New York.

I communicated with Bron almost every day. We talked about his home and hundreds of other planets he'd visited with his mind. I told him how much I loved the messenger pigeons.

Almost every day Liam and I would drive the birds farther and farther away from the loft; a different direction each day. They always made it home; most of the time before we did. I was up to fifty miles in half a year.

Bron asked me questions about the birds. Some of these were revealing of his alien nature.

Do they speak to you, friend Hogarth?

Do you mean like you and I, Bron? Like us putting down words on this computer screen?

Words?

Yes. Words.

I do not know what words are. Are you using words to communicate with me?

How do you express yourself to me, Bron?

I think into the last wisp of light from the Stelladron that once embraced my people. It translates my ideas to your device.

When you communicate with InfoMargins haven't you had to understand the concept of words?

I don't communicate with them the way I do with you, brother. I simply give directives.

How do you do that? I mean why would they listen to you?

The reason all humans listen . . . the potential to acquire value.

Money?

Just so.

But how did you get money here on Earth?

I imagined it existed and it did. Your machines are wonderful things. They hum a simple song that I can sing along with.

How much money did you imagine, Bron?

I have a mission for you, brother. Tomorrow you will stay at home and receive a cardboard box. You will take this box to a Union Express delivery service office and have it delivered to the address that will come in an envelope with the box.

What's in the box, Bron?

Nothing of any importance, friend Hogarth.

*T*HE NEXT MORNING THE BOX CAME. The man who brought it wore gray overalls with no insignia. He had a swarthy complexion that could have come from anywhere. He was a decade past handsome but his salt-and-pepper mustache was stylish and his eyes were dark.

"Where's this from?" I asked him.

He didn't answer.

"Who sent it?"

He smiled apologetically. Either he didn't speak English or he was told not to.

Bron didn't say for me not to open the carton and so I slit the binding tape with a serrated kitchen knife. The box contained twelve clear bottles made from thick glass. The bottles were separated from each other by wrapping bubbles and filled to their metal tops with clear liquid. The address was a post office box in St. Petersburg, Russia. I dithered around for three hours and then called Liam to take me to the Union Express office.

"Liam," I said on the way to the delivery office.

"Yes, Mr. Tryman."

"How long have you been driving limos?"

"Ever since I got out of the army. I was a commando you know."

"Where?"

"All over the world but I was in the U.S. Army," he said easily, his mild brogue in evidence. "They don't know a foot from an arse but they have good weapons and muscle to spare."

"When you were a soldier you took orders, right?"

"Yes, sir."

"Did you ever, ever disobey?"

He pulled the car to the curb in front of the delivery service office and sat there obviously considering my question.

"No," he said. "But then again I did things that I would na do again."

"Do you regret things you've done?"

He turned around putting his elbow on the back of his seat. He was wearing a yellow suit and a pale green shirt that day.

"Regrets are the easy way out. You shed a tear but the children who seen ya shed blood on their own land still suffer."

I thought he was going to say more but he didn't.

If I was at home I wouldn't have sent those bottles off. But there I was at the service already. I got out and sent Bron's package.

THAT NIGHT I SAT UP WORRYING about those bottles, about the poison they no doubt contained. Would wiping out a city in Russia somehow save jellyfish off the coast of Africa?

At four in the morning I messaged Bron.

What was in those bottles?

Water.

I don't believe you.

I am not lying, friend Hogarth.

Okay. I'm sorry. I just. I'm just worried.

Do not worry. Tend to your birds. Enjoy your wealth and your
friends.

I said okay and good-bye but I didn't believe my *friend*.
For the next week I looked up St. Petersburg on the Internet
a dozen times a day. After that I expanded my search through
all of Russia and then in the rest of the world looking for
sudden deadly contagions. Nothing showed up.

After twenty days of little to no sleep my fingertips began to go numb.

All this time I went on with my life, losing weight con-
stantly, seeing my few friends, and tending to my birds. My
pigeons were mostly snow white. A few had markings: a
black feather or a peacock blue collar. They also had per-
sonalities and other subtle differences. My favorite was
Dodger. He evaded me for the first few weeks when I tried
to grab him and put on his message clip. But after a while
he'd come to me cooing and cocking his head to look me in
the eye.

I had gone on four dates with Marla. We went to the
Bronx Zoo, Sag Harbor for an afternoon, the Metropoli-
tan Museum of Art, and finally to the Blue Note to hear the
fabulous bassist Ron Carter. We always took public trans-
portation or cabs wherever we went. I didn't want Marla to
know the extent of my newfound wealth. I just wanted to
be normal with her.

During a break between sets at the Blue Note Marla

reached across the table and took my hands. I could barely feel the touch due to the growing numbness.

"How come you never kiss me, Trent?" she said.

"I . . ."

"Don't you like me . . . like that?"

"I didn't want to be forward," I said. But that wasn't true. I had sent twelve quarts of deadly poison to Russia. What right did I have to kiss anyone?

"Can we go to your place after the music?"

I nodded, unable to speak, and Marla smiled. Maybe she thought I was shy. I had been timid before but that was all washed away. I was a mass murderer now. I was on the verge of becoming the greatest villain in the history of the world.

"IT'S OKAY," MARLA SAID when it became obvious that I could not achieve an erection. "You're just nervous."

I hadn't had an orgasm in weeks. I hadn't slept or eaten well or laughed or cried. All I could do was to wait for disaster. I put my arms around Marla's reassuring dark body and held her.

"You're cold," she whispered. "Maybe you're sick."

WHEN MARLA HAD FALLEN ASLEEP I got up and walked around my new apartment, the one Bron bought from Ralph Moore. The architect had taken out most of the walls of this upper unit and installed huge picture windows. The small bedroom and the toilet were walled off but the rest of the vast apartment, which took up the whole upper floor, was open, airy.

I wrapped myself in a terry-cloth bathrobe and went up to the roof.

My birds cooed for me and I relaxed a moment. I took out the special food Bron helped me acquire that helped the birds develop superior strength and intelligence. I climbed into the loft with them as they slept and jostled. I sat for hours among my birds shivering in the cold.

When the sun began rising I went back down to the apartment.

Marla was still asleep. One of the reasons she had asked to come to my place that night was because she didn't have to go to work the next day.

At 7:14 the doorbell rang. A delivery man brought in a box exactly like the one containing the bottles I had sent off to Russia.

This man was black and old, maybe seventy. He walked with a stooped-over gait.

"Tryman?" he asked after setting the heavy box down.

"Yeah."

"You should get a elevator in this building," the old man said. "It should be against the law not to have no elevators over three floors."

"Who sent this?"

"I don't know. I work for Dunster's Delivery. They got this box and said for me to take it with no paperwork. I asked them if that wasn't against the Patriot Act but they said they knew the guy."

I gave the man a ten-dollar tip and then put the box into

the closet across the way from the front door. This box would not go to Bron's destination.

"TRENT!" MARLA CALLED OUT as I slid up behind and entered her with my bone-hard erection.

I was so excited that it felt as if I couldn't stop bucking back and forth, in and out of her. I couldn't speak either.

"Do you have a condom on, baby?"

"Yeah," I huffed, stiff from my neck to my toes.

"Let me see!" She pushed back and then pulled away getting up to her knees.

I stayed on my side moving back and forth.

"You do have one on," she said, surprised.

"I want you," I said.

She pushed my shoulder and I was on my back; thin as a rail and straight as one too.

"Let me see it," she said.

Marla rolled the bright yellow condom off my black erection. She smiled holding her hands out around it, not touching me, seemingly amazed that it stood up on its own.

"You like me, Trent?"

I nodded and she brought her hands together around my cock. The moment she touched me I began ejaculating.

"Dog," Marla said. "Damn."

I kept coming, crying out for her to grab me hard but she just smiled moving her fingers gently against the over-sensitized skin.

"Does it feel good?" she asked.

I couldn't answer. I reached to hold myself but she held my hand back.

"You don't need no help with that, Trent."

I moaned then.

"You always come this much?"

"I've been thinking about you," I said.

"You must'a been thinkin' all mont'."

IN THE NEXT THREE MONTHS I received six more cartons. Each one I stacked in the closet. Marla and I developed a relationship but I managed to keep her from finding out about my job. I didn't let Liam drive me to work any longer and I told R.G. to keep an even lower profile.

I almost never slept.

I raised my birds and talked regularly to Bron but he never asked about the boxes after the first one and I never told him that I did not send them to Bamaco, Dijon, Galveston, Hong Kong, Jakarta, and Lima, Peru.

The sex I had with Marla was the best I'd ever known. I don't know how she felt about it. She would laugh at me after I'd come.

"Why do you laugh?" I once asked.

"You just get so excited," she said. "Sometimes I get worried that you might be havin' a heart attack or sumpin'."

"That makes you laugh?"

"I'm just happy you like me so much," she said, and then she kissed me.

THAT WAS A CRAZY PERIOD in my life. I had gone from fat to skinny, from traitor to my race to humanity's last hope, from data entry to VP. I think that it was Liam who turned me from Bron's Mission. The sadness in his voice and his refusal to wallow in regret . . .

In the end I was too small to contain the Mission to save God. Between my birds and my lover, Liam and R.G., Miguel and Hugo and Dora, I had become another man, a lesser man in many ways.

When I had made the decision to kill off humanity I felt big. I was more than anyone. I was willing to do something that no other villain had ever even imagined. I would kill everyone. I would do to mankind what they would do, albeit unawares, to uncounted dimensions.

But then I lost heart.

The boxes of poison stacked up in my closet. I didn't know what danger they posed so I couldn't throw them away or pour them down the drain.

After a year had passed, and boxes were stacked up to the closet ceiling, I never slept at all.

My vision was askew. Sometimes I'd stumble when walking.

"Why don't you sleep, baby?" Marla would ask when I'd be sitting up in the bed at night.

"I'm going through a transition at work," I'd say.

After a few nights of her pulling me down next to her I became good at pretending to sleep. I'd lie there listening to her gentle breathing, trying to figure out how it was that Bron planned to trick me.

Every night I would lay in bed, with or without Marla, my body thrumming from the lack of sleep and nutrition. I lived on candy bars and French fries. I should have gained weight but my body refused to digest the food. None of this bothered me. I'd accepted my fate. I was going to die and die soon but first I would figure out Bron's plan and, somehow, stymie him.

But even here there was a contradiction—I still loved the Stelladren. I had only seen them once but their beauty was beyond anything I could imagine. They weren't life like I was. They were a coming together of all sentience, far beyond the petty mucus of human potential. They were raised above me like Jesus stepping over horse dung.

But for all the love I felt for the Stelladren I could not kill Marla and Miguel.

My mother sent me brief messages of love and religious sentiment every other day and I had Liam return her pigeons.

I gave pigeons to all my friends and we communicated regularly with Liam running back and forth, returning the birds to their owners for future messages.

I asked Miguel via pigeon to get me a pistol. We never spoke about it. He just brought the gun to school one day, put it in a company pouch, and had it sent by interoffice mail to my desk. It was a .38 pistol, loaded and ready to fire.

I had come to think during my long nights of vampirelike repose that Bron must have needed me for some specific reason. He had all kinds of power without me. He controlled businesses and the lives of thousands. If he could deliver the bottles of poison to me then he could have sent them to their destinations around the world.

Maybe the bottles were a distraction. Maybe he had something else in mind. But regardless Bron had chosen me for a reason. He had put me in place so that I would do something to ensure his plans against humanity.

It came to me on a Wednesday that my death might be

the only way to halt Bron's machinations. He seemed to want to keep me alive. I had a bodyguard and a driver. Maybe if I killed myself at some important juncture I would be saving the human race.

LIFE FOR ME was like a beautiful and terrible dream for most of that year. I was rich and powerful, thin and protected. My lover believed that she knew me . . . and she did—except for my relationship with Bron. I went to work every day and saw Marla four nights a week. I told her everything about my life up to Bron's intervention. Then I only made vague references to a small promotion for years of service.

I communicated with Bron almost every day. Our *talks* were meaningless—I knew. I was torn up inside over my betrayal of the Stelladren. They were magnificent beings, conduits to God. Their ultimate deaths would accompany my own I knew. This knowledge was the only reason I had not yet taken my life.

ONE NIGHT I SAT UP, suddenly aware that my birds were part of Bron's plan. He had asked me to get them; that was his first request after agreeing to let some portion of the human race survive. At three in the morning I went up on the roof with a butcher's knife planning to kill all of Bron's messengers of death. I reached in and grabbed my favorite, Dodger, by his neck. He squawked but I just pressed his beak up with my thumb and slit his throat with a deep thrust. A drop of hot blood spurted out onto my cheek and the bird fluttered wildly for much longer than I would have thought possible.

After Dodger died I stood there on my roof paralyzed with a dead pigeon in one hand and the murder weapon in the other. My fingers and feet and face were all numb. I could feel the blood moving painfully in my veins.

When the sky began to lighten I went down to my old apartment and rooted around until I found a packet of note cards that my mother had given me many years ago—before I went to work for Shiloh Statistics. They were cream colored with my name printed in blue across the top: HOGARTH TRYMAN. The only printed evidence left of my real name.

Dear Marla,

It is because I love you that I cannot see you again. I am a very very bad person. I have done terrible things. I have murdered and covered it up. I have betrayed everyone. I have plotted against my fellow man and I can no longer live with it. I love you and I always will in threads of light from a dark dark sea.

Trent "Hogarth" Tryman

I sealed the note into an envelope, placed a stamp upon it, and addressed it to the diner. I took the pistol from a drawer and put it in my pocket.

I mailed the letter not three blocks from my apartment planning to kill myself then and there. But instead I started walking in the dawning light. I was going to kill myself on the street so that everyone could see me. Bron couldn't get at me if I was dead, maybe then his plans would be undone. I was weak and staggery, tingling, numb, thrumming, and

deeply rueful over the murder of Dodger and the fate my
decision would have across the planes of existence.

Twice I walked in front of cars heedless of the stoplights
but alert drivers managed to hit their brakes before slam-
ming into me. As the morning grew thousands of people
flooded the streets with their noise and their ignorance.

My forearms were trembling.

My heart felt like a thirsty dog's tongue lapping up
water.

I know that I must have been talking to myself because
people were staring at me, moving out of my way. This made
me laugh. In a moment of intuition I realized that this was
how I had felt about myself for years: a mumbling loser
walking down the streets shunned by anyone who saw me
coming—my mother and the newspaper vendor, the dog
walker and the dog—by everyone except Bron who only
wanted to use me.

"I'm the killer!" I shouted.

A woman walking past me jumped and yelped.

"I have killed and I would kill again."

Men and women moved away from me and even though
I understood why I was still enraged that they were not listening.

I pulled out my .38 and people began running.

"Watch out!" a man shouted and I shot him for not urg-
ing people to pay attention.

I laughed at him looking at me with shock in his eyes. I
didn't mean to laugh. I knew that the papers and the news
would report that "the madman laughed as he shot his victims."

People were yelling, running. I backed around in a tight

circle shooting now and then. I was dizzy and feeling drunk.
When the bullets were all gone I decided to walk on. There
were people lying on the sidewalk around me. I would walk
until someone killed me. That would show Bron.

I WOKE UP IN A WHITE ROOM, in a big bed, in a straightjacket, alone. I was very tired and my head hurt. I appreciated
the restraints. Maybe that would keep me from destroying
the world.

I fell asleep.

When I woke up a dour-faced nurse was checking my
temperature. She had violet eyes, I remember.

"Like Liz Taylor," I said but either she didn't hear me or
she had no desire to respond.

I fell asleep.

When I came to awareness again I was sitting in a chair,
still in the straightjacket. Across a white table from me sat
three people: a man and two women, all in business attire.

The man introduced himself as my lawyer, Jack Wor-
man. The women were Ellen Barge, a pudgy state prosecu-
tor, and Alana Tidyman, a psychiatrist.

My lips were numb and my tongue felt quite thick and
dry.

Tidyman, who was petite and bright eyed, started asking me questions. And even though I found it difficult to
talk I tried my best.

She asked me what had led up to the shootings.

I told her about the instant messages and Bron and getting my job. I told her about the Scarlet Death and my un-
witting implication in it.

"You believe that someone over the Internet made you shoot those people in the street?" my lawyer asked.

"No," I said. "I just got carried away after killing Dodger."

"The pigeon?"

"I can prove that Bron is plotting worldwide destruction," I said. "Just look in the closet in my apartment. There are bottles filled with poison there. Toxins so powerful that they could wipe out half the globe."

The three glanced at each other and then back at me.

"No one told you to kill the people on the street?" Tidyman asked.

"They wouldn't listen," I said. "I was trying to warn them."

"Why did you have the gun?"

"To kill myself before I killed everyone else."

"Then why did you shoot those people?"

I knew what the reason was but I didn't have the words to make it clear. I thought at the time it was because of the numbness, maybe drugs they had given me, but I came later to know that I was insane, that I had lost my mind.

The people went away and I was wheeled back to my room. I slept a lot over the next period of time. I didn't have any way of judging how many days had passed.

Now and again a nurse would come in and feed me. I didn't mind the helplessness.

After six or seven feedings and half as many sleep periods a tall man in a dark blue suit came to see me.

He had russet-colored hair and a pencil-thin brown mustache. The air around this man seemed to bristle with energy.

"Hello, Hogarth," he said. "My name is Justin Mack."

I was surprised to hear him say my given name but almost immediately I remembered the card to Marla.

"How's Marla?" I asked.

"Who?" He looked puzzled a moment and then serious again. "Bron sent me."

Something happened when he mention Bron's name. It took me a moment to realize that I had stopped breathing. Was this man behind some elaborate scheme? Had he somehow fooled me into believing in God?

But then I thought about the three who had questioned me. I had told them Bron's name and my given name, for that matter.

"I've come to help you," Justin Mack said.

"Help me what?"

"I'm taking you home."

"Home?" I said. "I'm going to jail for murder."

"No one died," he said reassuringly, "and InfoMargins has taken full responsibility for your mental breakdown. We can take you home today."

"And you say you know Bron?"

"Of course, Hogarth. How do you think you got made VP? Your friend owns InfoMargins and uses me to make things happen."

"But what about the bottles?" I asked.

"What bottles?"

"The ones in the boxes in my closet?"

"Water," he said, making a dismissive gesture with his lips.

I hated him at that moment.

"A male nurse is going to get you out of this jacket," Mack continued, "and then Robert George will come with an officer of the court to put an electronic ankle bracelet on you. Then they'll take you home. You can stay there until our psychiatrists can declare you sane again."

"No trial?"

"You were insane at the time of the commission of the crimes. Six months house arrest, weekly visits with a psychiatrist, and you'll be free."

IT ALL HAPPENED just as he said. R.G. was very nice to me as was the policeman who helped put me in the wheelchair.

On the ride back to my apartment Liam told me that he had fed my birds. I was happy that only Dodger had died.

When I got home I logged on and sent a message out to Bron but he didn't answer. I looked up my crimes on the Internet.

I'd only shot three people and none of them was seriously injured. Justin Mack had admitted that he'd promoted me to my position as a kind of misguided attempt to make his companies more racially integrated and at the same time prove his position that anyone could be a manager in the workplace given the proper support.

He apologized publicly and had given each wounded individual ten million dollars.

There were many lawsuits but the public outcry was diminishing quickly.

The phone rang while I was reading about myself.

"Hello?"

"Hi, baby."

"Marla . . ."

"Don't you wanna talk to me?"

"I do but didn't you get my note?"

"You were outta your mind," she said in a satisfying Southern tone. "It's just lucky you didn't kill anybody."

"You're not mad at me?" I asked.

"No, honey. But I do wonder why you didn't tell me that you had such a big job."

"I don't know," I said. "I guess I just wanted you to like me for me."

"Can I come over and show you how much I like you?"

BEFORE MARLA GOT THERE Miguel called to wish me well. He thanked me without saying why but I knew that it was because I didn't tell anyone about how I got the .38.

My mother called.

"What kind of mother am I?" she asked me.

"What do you mean, Mom?"

"I mean how did I make a son so crazy that he goes out in the street shooting at people?"

I COULDN'T MAKE LOVE AGAIN but Marla was very sweet about it. She stroked my head where a man named Alfred Armstrong had hit me after he was sure that I was out of bullets.

I woke up in the middle of the night trying to understand what was happening. Most of it didn't make sense. Justin Mack said that he worked for Bron but that didn't mean Bron was an alien mind loose in the world. The Scarlet Death had happened. I had almost died from the disease. But that was a terrestrial infection, not something from space or beyond space.

Maybe I was crazy after all. If I was insane that would also explain the meteorite. Maybe I thought I remembered the meteorite but in reality it was a hallucination I had *after* the news reported it . . .

What had happened refused to make sense. And what I believed was beyond imagination.

In the living room of the new apartment I stood naked against the window, looking down on the rainy street. I'd lost weight, lots of it, but my muscles were atrophied so my flesh still sagged like a fat man's. I had confessed to all of my crimes but no one believed me.

Bron had abandoned me.

And still I felt that I was a linchpin in a bomb. All I had to do was move one way or another and the world would come crashing down around the ears of history.

A woman hurried by on the dark street holding an umbrella against the storm. She rushed under me unaware that I held her future in my hands.

Or maybe I was just crazy.

I went naked into the stairwell of the top floor and ascended to the roof. It was cold and wet, of course, it was raining after all. The drugs I was taking allowed me to know that it was cold without feeling it. I grinned up there on my roof.

My roof. This was the only piece of evidence that made sense to me. My roof. I was a fat, black, data entry clerk not a skinny rich man who owned a roof looking down on Gramercy Park. I was never interested in messenger pigeons or willing to commit murder or suicide.

The fact that I stood upon that roof proved that alien life existed and had contacted me. The fact that Justin Mack, one of the most powerful white men in the world, publicly apologized for me verified the existence of God.

My laughter was swallowed by the strident hiss of rain-fall.

I peered into my pigeons' loft. They were aware of me. Dozens of red eyes glistened in the dark looking for the cause of the sound at their walls.

The loft was made from four sections. Each was a four-sided wall with a triangular quarter part of the roof tilted inward. The four walls were held together by simple rods of steel. All I had to do to release them was twist and pull.

The storm roared pelting me with hard raindrops that would have hurt if I hadn't been drugged.

One wall fell, then another, then the last two. My white pigeons, forty-seven of them now that Dodger was dead, moved nervously, hating the rain and wind.

The roar of the storm was joined by another sound, one that I could not quite make out.

"Get the fuck out of here you stupid birds!" I yelled into the wind. "I don't want you. I never wanted you. I'm going back to the way it was."

The birds huddled together and then cried out, making a noise that no pigeons had ever made before. The sound in the sky was a plane, a jet engine. As one the birds took wing and swirled upward in the form of a corkscrew. It was a fantastic sight.

As I watched them I saw huge yellow lights softened by the darkness and the clouds. The swirl of birds was swallowed up into the darkness and light and a sound like the sputtering of giant lips made its way to my ears.

Sensation ceased then. There was no rain or wind or roar. There was nothing at all; nothing except for the feeling of motion—not walking or flying or falling but more like focusing on a place far away on a higher, clearer level.

"Hogarth."

It was day now and I was on a steep mountain path. The trees around me had bright red trunks and writhing blue leaves. The ground was alive with pink and blue insect-like creatures that swarmed over my feet without biting.

Down maybe twenty feet away was tall manlike being whose slender shoulders were no wider than his graceful head. He was violet and semitransparent, both liquid and burning. I couldn't make out his features.

"Bron?"

"We meet at last."

"This is where you were born?"

"Walk toward me," the man-thing made from molten blood and air said.

"What are these bugs doing?" I asked.

"Learning you. Walk toward me."

"What happened?" I asked, afraid to move. "Where am I?"

"Walk toward me and you will see what I see," Bron said. "You will know what I know."

"Stay there, man," I said.

The words I spoke reminded me of Miguel and suddenly he was standing there next to me. Every detail of his appearance was perfect. I had conjured him.

"Walk toward me," Bron said and Miguel disappeared.

"Talk to me first," I said.

"Words are lies, friend Hogarth. They cannot give knowledge but only refer to it—words are charlatans."

"What do you mean?"

"Walk toward me."

I took a step and stopped.

Bron did the same.

I thought of my mother then. She had loved my father and he left her with me. My father, Rhineking Tryman, was a deep black river and my mother and I were its opposite shores. The sadness of this revelation nearly devastated me.

"Walk toward me."

I took a step and so did Bron. As we approached each other the insects scuttled off my naked, sagging brown calfs. Bron and I were face to face and we took another step . . .

We only touched and our beings were fully merged. I knew this instinctively. I could see the Stelladren as they were: huge fleshy prisms that guided the energies of Soul. I was there in the hot core of a single tendril. I was there and so was Bron and billions upon billions of others.

I knew Bron's history. His father's battle with a tree gone insane with flames. I knew his peoples' history: the blending of the hot core of his planet with a virus-laden sky.

I could see with Bron's receptors how he saw time. All around me were a thousand possibilities; a clear day, a cloudy one, a landscape filled with gala (the pink and blue bugs), a day when the gala rested. It was all the same day. I could choose between these possibilities and blend them.

There was a feeling of deep ecstasy in me at that moment. I could see, physically, through time itself. How I held my body, just how I breathed could change what would be.

I turned this vision upon myself . . .

It was then that the terrible plan of Bron became apparent.

There was a focal point for Bron's vision. It was me on that rooftop in the rain throwing back the walls of the loft after my birds had spent a year eating certain proteins that would drive them insane while at the same time giving them extraordinary strength.

"But why?"

"You were the only one," Bron said.

"You didn't need me. You could have contacted anyone through computers." But even as I said it I realized that my connection with Bron had only been on the computer in the beginning. After the Scarlet Death, after I had *seen* the Stelladren on what I thought was my television I had been connected with the alien directly. I was linked to him through that tendril of light and flesh.

"We needed you on that roof at that moment," said Bron. "No one else could have done what you did at precisely the right instant. Time is like a dance and every motion is unique though not necessarily predestined."

"So you used me," I said or thought or felt.

"I am one with you, friend Hogarth. We are together on my home world, united. Can't you see that this has to happen? This is the only way in all the visions of all futures that will ensure the longevity of the Universal Soul."

"But so many will die."

"They are, as we are, part of a greater whole."

"They will suffer and die," I said. I wanted to scream but I couldn't.

"As my race suffered and died," Bron said.

I could see the beings of fire and air dissipating all over his planet. When their connection to the Stelladron was severed they died by the billions. I could feel the loss of their entire history.

"Because they died you will kill us?" I asked Bron, myself.

"It is not revenge we seek, friend Hogarth. It is equilibrium. The future will be bleak without the Stelladren to guide the shards of our souls. You know this, you see it through me."

"But you lied to me, Bron."

"I brought you here."

THE SUN WAS OUT when I woke up on the white sofa in the big room of my upper apartment. Marla was shaking my shoulder.

"Baby, baby, wake up," she said. But she said other things too. *It's terrible* and *we all gonna die* and *it's the end of the world, baby.* I could see her in different poses and positions. Sometimes she wore a dressing gown and other times not. But no matter when I saw her she was in distress.

I decided to concentrate on one image. The most likely one.

"There's a world war goin' on," she said. "A jet plane from New York crashed near Washington and some missiles got fired. Los Angeles is gone and Paris and Beijing, Seattle and Moscow. There's a dozen cities destroyed all over the world. You think we should try and get outta New York?"

"No," I said. "It's going to be all right."

"All right!" she yelled. "All right! Are you crazy? They dyin' all ovah the world!"

"Calm down, Marla," I said getting to my feet. "The phone is going to ring and you're going to answer it. It will be Justin Mack."

As the last word came from my lips the phone rang. Marla, in a state of shock, answered.

"Hello?" she said. She listened for a moment and then, "He wants to talk to you," she told me.

She handed me the phone. I delayed a few seconds before taking it and a few moments more before speaking.

"Mr. Mack."

"Hogarth?"

"Yes, Justin. Bron says for you to call on the president. Tell him that we need to start sending antibiotics and antivirals to China. Tell him that the problem isn't nuclear holocaust but diseases set free by the volley of attack. The jetliner that crashed in the secret Pentagon center disrupted the switching of target codes for our missile system. Don't ask why the Pentagon would have American targets in their system just accept it. We're lucky that some American cities were hit. That way our armed neighbors will be willing to understand and forgive."

"Forgive? There's at least twenty-five million dead," Mack said. I could tell by his voice, and my fractured temporal vision, that he was about to break down.

"Over four billion will die before this is over, Justin," I said, choosing my words to keep him in the realm of sanity. "Everyone will unless you call the president now."

"What will I say to him?"

"Tell him that I called you," I said. "Tell him that I told you the code words for targeting D.C. are 'raging fool.' Tell him that in seventeen hours messages will start coming in about a powerful infection eating its way down the Yellow River Valley. He won't be able to contain it but he will retard it enough to keep it from completely wiping out humanity. That's all, Justin. That's your place in history."

I pressed the off button on the phone and closed my eyes. Possibilities flooded through my mind. I was no longer seeing the world but intuiting it through a sense mechanism that Bron passed on to me before he died.

It was only then that I realized that Bron was dead. I tried to mourn him but he was so alive inside of me that I could not bring myself to feel the loss.

I heard Marla say something in the near future.

"No, honey," I said. "We have to stay here."

"I need to get down to either my mother in Atlanta or my daddy in Miami," she said in the present, regarding me with growing fear.

"Florida will be taken over by Cuban troops before the day is over," I said. "They'll be worried that the U.S. will turn its army on them. And if you try to get down to Georgia you'll be killed by one of the gangs forming along the highways between the cities. It won't be safe for three months."

"But they gonna blow up New York!" Marla clasped her hands pumping them up and down as if hammering at a stake.

I reached out to her down a dozen paths of possibility. But in each of these she left for her family. Finally I looked down on her journey. I saw her raped and sodomized, beaten and murdered. I searched and searched until I saw the one chance she had.

"Marla."

"I got to go," she said.

She tried to move but I grabbed her hands.

"Listen to me," I said. "You have a pistol in the hatbox in your closet, right?"

"How you know that?"

"If you meet a man with a scar under a dead eye kill him with that gun. Kill him the moment you see him. If you do that you may live."

I let her go and she waited a moment staring at me. It was the closest chance for her to stay in the comparative safety of New York. But I could see her leaving later and that road led only to death.

"Good-bye, Trent."

"Hogarth," I said, correcting her. "If you live call me Hogarth son of Rhineking."

Watching her leave I could see the paths of my life changing with the departure. Our son Clyde who would not be born. Our Southern California house with the pomegranate tree in the front yard that would never be built.

Through the last living tendril of the Stelladron that connected Bron's mind with mine I could see, with his temporal sight, a thousand thousand possibilities. I had to pull my sight back so that I could perceive waves of possibility, not focusing on individual time lines. In this way I could cull out the best possible influences that I could have on the world.

I could see possible pasts and their probable futures. I

could see my part in the annihilation of at least half of the human race. I felt remorse but not guilt. I was only a player and yet without me humanity would have perished.

It was my destiny to be where I was and what I was. I would protect the Stelladren and save as much of humanity as possible. Marla would probably die as would my mother of a heart attack and Miguel and Liam in the Battle of Tampa. I couldn't save my friends. I couldn't save the billions around the globe who were destined to die. But I could save the millions that had a chance.

I was to be the savior of a world that I had ushered into ruin.

I would have preferred death but that was not to be. Everyone who was to know my secret would hate me and still give their lives to keep my power alive. I was evil. I was necessary, vital. My name would ultimately achieve sainthood across the universe and my soul would be damned among the people whose lives I both saved and destroyed.

Merge

ALSO BY WALTER MOSLEY

LEONID McGILL MYSTERIES
All I Did Was Shoot My Man
When the Thrill Is Gone
Known to Evil
The Long Fall

EASY RAWLINS MYSTERIES
Blonde Faith
Cinnamon Kiss
Little Scarlet
Six Easy Pieces
Bad Boy Brawly Brown
A Little Yellow Dog
Black Betty
Gone Fishin'
White Butterfly
A Red Death
Devil in a Blue Dress

OTHER FICTION
The Tempest Tales
Diablerie
Killing Johnny Fry
*The Gift of Fire / On the Head
    of a Pin*
The Man in My Basement

Fear of the Dark
Fortunate Son
The Wave
Fear Itself
Futureland
Fearless Jones
Walkin' the Dog
Blue Light
*Always Outnumbered, Always
    Outgunned*
RL's Dream
47
The Right Mistake
The Last Days of Ptolemy Grey

NONFICTION
*Twelve Steps Toward Political
    Revelation*
This Year You Write Your Novel
*What Next: A Memoir Toward
    World Peace*
Life Out of Context
Workin' on the Chain Gang

PLAYS
The Fall of Heaven

WALTER MOSLEY

CROSSTOWN TO OBLIVION

Merge

TOR®

A TOM DOHERTY ASSOCIATES BOOK • NEW YORK

MERGE / DISCIPLE

Copyright © 2012 by Walter Mosley

Illustrations by Greg Ruth

A Tor Book
Published by Tom Doherty Associates, LLC
175 Fifth Avenue
New York, NY 10010

www.tor-forge.com

Tor® is a registered trademark of Tom Doherty Associates, LLC.

ISBN 978-0-7653-3009-3 (hardcover)
ISBN 978-1-4299-8826-1 (e-book)

First Edition: October 2012

Printed in the United States of America

0 9 8 7 6 5 4 3 2 1

In honor of PKD

ACKNOWLEDGMENTS

For my good friend Diane Houslin

Merge

There ain't no blues like the sky.

IT WASN'T THERE a moment before and then it was, in my living room at seven sixteen in the evening on Tuesday, December the twelfth, two thousand seven. I thought at first it was a plant, a dead plant, a dead branch actually, leaning up against the wall opposite my desk. I tried to remember it being there before. I'd had many potted shrubs and bushes in my New York apartment over the years. They all died from lack of sun. Maybe this was the whitewood sapling that dropped its last glossy green leaf just four months after I bought it, two weeks before my father died. But no, I remembered forcing that plant down the garbage chute in the hall.

Just as I was about to look away the branch seemed to quiver. The chill up my spine was strong enough to make me flinch.

"What the hell?"

I could make out a weak hissing sound in the air. Maybe that sound was what made me look up in the first place. It

was a faltering exhalation, like a man in the process of dying in the next room or the room beyond that.

I stood up from the seventeenth set of lectures in the eighth volume of *The Popular Educator Library* and moved, tentatively, toward the shuddering branch.

My apartment was small and naturally dark but I had six-hundred-watt incandescent lamps, specially made for construction sites, set up in opposite corners. I could see quite clearly that the branch was not leaning against the wall but standing, swaying actually, on a root system that was splayed out at its base like the simulation of a singular broad foot.

The shock of seeing this wavering tree limb standing across from me had somehow short-circuited my fear response. I moved closer, wondering if it was some kind of serpent that one of my neighbors had kept for a pet. Could snakes stand up straight like that?

The breathing got louder and more complex as I approached.

I remember thinking, *Great, I win the lotto only to be killed by a snake nine months later.* Maybe I should have done what Nicci told me and moved to a nice place on the Upper West Side. I had the money: twenty-six million over twenty years. But I didn't want to move right off. I wanted to take it slowly, to understand what it meant to be a million-aire, to never again worry about work or paying the bills.

The sound was like the hiss of a serpent but I didn't see eyes or a proper mouth. Maybe it was one of those South American seed drums that someone had put there to scare me.

"Nicci?" I called into the bedroom even though I knew she couldn't be there. "Nicci, are you in there?"

No answer. She had sent my key back two years before—a little while after she left me for Thomas Beam.

Even though I was facing this strange hissing branch the thought of Tom Beam brought back the stinging memory of Nicci asking me if I minded if she went out to a show with him.

"He's just a friend," she'd said. "He's not interested in me or anything like that."

And then, two months later, after we had made love in my single bed her saying, "I've been sleeping with Tommy for six weeks, Rahl."

"What?"

"We've been fucking, all right?" she said as if I had been the one to say something to make *her* angry.

"What does this mean?" I asked.

I knew that she hadn't been enjoying sex with me. I knew that she was getting ready to go back to college and finish her degree in business; that she was always telling me that I could do better than the filing job I had with the Bendman and Lowell Accounting Agency.

"Do you love him?" I asked.

"I don't know."

"Are you going to keep seeing him?"

"For a while," Nicci Charbon said. "What do you want?"

It was just after midnight and my penis had shrunk down to the size of a lima bean; the head had actually pulled back into my body. My palms started itching, so much so that I scratched at them violently.

"What's wrong?" Nicci asked.

"What's wrong? You just told me that you're fucking Tommy Beam."

"You don't have to use foul language," she said.

"But you said the word first."

"I did not."

We went back and forth on that fine point until Nicci said, "Well what if I did say it? You're the one who told me it was all right to go out with him."

"I . . ." It was then that I lost heart. Nicci Charbon was the most beautiful girl . . . woman I had ever known. I was amazed every morning I woke up next to her and surprised whenever she smiled to see me.

"I don't want to lose you, Nicci," I said. I wanted to ask her to come back to me but that seemed like a silly thing to say when we were in bed together in the middle of the night.

"You don't care about me and Tommy?" she asked.

"I don't want you to see him."

It was the first bit of backbone I showed. Nicci got sour faced, turned her back, and pretended to sleep.

I tried to talk to her but she said that she was too upset to talk. I said that I was the one that should have been upset. She didn't answer that.

I sat there awake until about three. After that I got dressed and went down to Milo's All Night Diner on Lexington. I ordered coffee and read yesterday's newspaper, thought about Nicci doing naked things with Tom Beam and listened to my heart thudding sometimes slowly, sometimes fast.

When I got back at six Nicci was gone. She'd left a note saying that it would probably be better if we didn't see each

other for a while. I didn't speak to her again for fifteen months. Most of that time I was in pain. I didn't talk about it all that much because there was no one to talk to and also because we were at war and a broken heart seems less important when you have peers that are dying from road-side landmines.

And then I won the lotto. Nicci called me three days after it was announced.

"No," she said when I asked about her new boyfriend. "I don't see Tommy all that much anymore. We were hot and heavy there at first but then I started college and he went to work for Anodyne down in Philly."

She called me every day for two weeks before I agreed to see her. We had lunch together and I didn't kiss her when we parted. She wanted to see me again but I said we could talk on the phone.

I wanted to see her, that was for sure. She looked very beautiful when we got together for lunch at Milo's. She wore a tight yellow dress and her makeup made her wolf-gray eyes glow with that same hungry look that they had the first night she came up to my place.

But what was I supposed to do? Nicci had dropped me like an anchor, cut the rope, and sailed off with another man.

And now there was this seed drum or serpent hissing in my room.

A four-inch slit opened in the stick toward where the head would be if it was a snake or a man. The opening was the length of a human mouth, only it was vertical and lip-less. A rasping breath came from the thing and I heard something else; a sound, a syllable.

I saw then that it couldn't have been a stick because it was undulating slightly, the brown limb showing that it was at least somewhat supple—supporting the snake theory.

I leaned forward ignoring the possible danger.

"Foo," the limb whispered almost inaudibly.

I fell back bumping against the desk and knocking my nineteen-forties' self-study college guide to the floor. It was a talking stick, a hungry branch. Sweat broke out across my face and for the first time in nearly two years I was completely unconcerned with Nicci Charbon and Thomas Beam.

"What?" I said in a broken voice.

"Food," the voice said again, stronger now, in the timbre of a child.

"What are you?"

"Food, please," it said in a pleading tone.

"What, what do you eat?"

"Thugar, fruit . . ."

My living room had a small kitchen in the corner. There was a fruit plate on the counter with a yellow pear, two green apples, and a bruised banana that was going soft. I grabbed the pear and an apple and approached the talking stick. I held the apple up to the slit in the woodlike skin. When the fruit was an inch from the opening three white tubes shot out piercing the skin.

The apple throbbed gently and slowly caved in on itself. After a few minutes it was completely gone. The tiny pale tubes ended in oblong mouthlike openings that seemed to be chewing. When they were finished they pulled back into the fabulous thing.

"More?" I asked.

"Yeth."

The creature ate all my fruit. When it had finished with the banana, peel and all, it slumped forward falling into my arms. It was a heavy beast, eighty pounds at least, and warmer by ten degrees than my body temperature. I hefted it up carrying it awkwardly like the wounded hero does the heroine in the final scene of an old action film.

I placed the thing upon my emerald-colored vinyl-covered couch and watched it breathing heavily through its vibrating slit of a mouth.

The living branch was round in body, four and half feet long. It was evenly shaped except for the bottom that spread out like a foot formed from a complex root system. The vertical slit was open wide sucking in air and it seemed to be getting hotter.

"Are you okay?" I asked, feeling a little foolish.

"Yessss."

"Do you need anything?"

"Resssst."

For a brief moment a white spot appeared at the center of the brown tube.

It gave the impression of being an eye, watching me for a moment, and then it receded into the body of the creature as its tubular mouths had done.

"Ressst," it said again.

I SAT AT THE COFFEE TABLE, a few feet away from the sofa, trying to figure out what had happened. One moment it wasn't there and then it was as if it had always been, hadn't come from anywhere. I didn't understand and I had no one to talk to that I could trust.

Nicci was gone and my only real friends, Pete and Frank, were angry with me for one reason or another.

"What's wrong wit' you, niggah?" Pete had said, spittle popping from his mouth. "Here you got all that cash and now you wanna ack like you don't know me."

Pete wanted a loan for the down payment on a house in Jersey City. But as long as I had known the big man, as many ones and fives and tens as I had loaned him over the years, he had never paid back a nickel or a dime. I told him that.

"But this is different, man," he said. "Now you got millions."

"It's the same old thing, Pete," I told him. "I got the money and you want it."

"Make sense, niggah," Pete said to me at Milo's counter.

Whenever he got mad he used what they call "the N word." I didn't mind. He and Frank and I were all black men. We'd come from the streets of the East Village. We called each other niggah ten times, a hundred and ten times a day.

"You got all that money, man," Pete said. "You got to get up off'a some'a that for your friends."

"I'm not buyin' *myself* a house, Pete."

"Buy me one then."

That was the last time we saw each other. He stopped calling me and I didn't call him because I didn't want to be used as his blank check.

Frank said that he didn't want anything from me and that was true; at least nothing like money. But just like Pete, Frank stopped talking to me.

I called his house a dozen times trying to get his advice about Pete but he wouldn't come to the phone. Hilda, his

girlfriend, would get on the line and say, "He's not here right now, Raleigh. I'll tell him you called."

But he was there, sitting in his deep red recliner watching football or some other sport. Frank was a sports addict, a self-professed expert on anything from soccer to boxing, tennis to basketball. I could hear the TV in the background. And I knew Hilda hated watching a game.

Finally one day Frank answered—by mistake, I guess.

"Hello."

"Frank?"

For three seconds there he was going to hang up I was sure. But he collected himself.

"What you want, Rahl?"

"I, I just wanted to talk, Frank."

"I'm busy."

"Why you don't answer my calls, man?" I asked.

"Did you quit your job?" he asked and I understood what had happened.

Frank had been dubbed "the guru" in high school. He was the one that many and most kids went to for advice. From pregnant girls to gang-related difficulties, Frank was always weighing in.

When I'd won the lotto he'd called and asked me to lunch. That was something in itself because Frank rarely called anybody. You had to call him.

"So what you gonna do, Rahl?" he asked me over iceberg lettuce and ranch dressing.

"What you mean, Frank?"

"Now you got all that money what are you planning to do?"

"I don't know, man. You know I got a sister someplace

and I always felt bad because I didn't do what my English teacher Mr. Montcalm said and tried to go to CCNY. I mean I got all that money comin' to me but it don't mean nuthin' if I stay just as stupid as I was before I got it."

"You aren't college material, Rahl," Frank said with certainty. "You got some good grades sometimes but you never applied yourself in high school. You read a book now and then but not like a college man. It's mostly just mysteries and crazy stories. What you should do is get yourself a financial planner and stay on the job. Keep on the steady doin' what you doin' and things'll work out."

"You mean just act like nuthin' happened and visit my money sometimes?"

Frank was an unattractive man, he had big ears and mottled skin from serious childhood acne. He was thin and bony too but he held himself like royalty. Women went crazy for him and his approbation and opinion were sought after in school, on the street, and by fellow workers at any job he held.

"You aren't gonna discover the cure for cancer or anything, Rahl," he said. "College just be a waste'a time for somebody like you."

"I don't wanna go to college, Frank," I complained. "My dad left me these books. *The Popular Educator Library*. It's fifteen hundred lectures on everything from accounting to zoology. I was thinking that I could stay up in my house and read those books and then I'd know what people were talking about and what the newspapers were sayin' for real."

"What difference would that make?"

"It make a difference to me. In my mind, you know?"

"Don't get me wrong, Rahl, but your daddy was a drunk and a fool . . ."

Maybe Frank hadn't been the first one to break off communication after all. As I sat there next to the shuddering, wheezing branch I remembered how angry I was that my childhood friend had dissed my father.

My father.

"RAHL," FRIEND REDMAN, my father, had said to me from his deathbed in a small East Side sanatorium.

"Yeah, Dad?"

"I got them books over at Sheila's house in a box that says 'cigars.' If anything happens to me she knows to get 'em to ya."

"Okay," I said. I was man of twenty-six years but I wanted to cry.

"I always meant to read them books," he said. "I, I knew that if I read 'em that I'd be a smarter man and, and, and a bettah man because you know a education is what makes men bettah in this world. And if I read it in a book nobody could claim that they taught me, that it was them and not me bein' so smart."

He was blind by that time. Something to do with the alcohol. He reached out and I took his hand.

"You should read them books, Raleigh. Read 'em from cover to cover. It's the best I can do for you, son."

AND SO WHEN FRANK CALLED my father a drunk and a fool he made sure that I was going to read those books.

Every word. Every article. Frank had no reason to talk about my father like he did.

"SURE I QUIT MY JOB," I said when I caught Frank on the phone that day. "Wouldn't I be a fool to work for minimum wage when I'm making over thirty-five hundred dollars a day from the lotto?"

Frank hung up on me. That was nearly a year before the tree limb showed up in my living room from the Gulf Between Worlds. The end of our relationship had been a mutual decision.

I guess I never felt all that good with Frank and Pete, it was just that they were my only friends and being with them was better than watching TV alone.

I PULLED UP a straight-back chair next to the couch and stared at the odd being. It was asleep or seemed to be, shaking slightly. I put a hand against the fleshlike log. It was vibrating. I felt this first in my hand and then up through my arm and shoulder. This pulsation entered my mind and suddenly I was nowhere.

I WASN'T ASLEEP nor had I lost consciousness. But my eyes were closed and I wasn't feeling things but only seeing a dizzyingly fast succession of images that seemed to originate from inside my mind.

This went on for a long while before my mind's eye settled on a singular tableau.

I was eating boiled figs and fresh watermelons, baked pineapples and stewed prunes. After eating all I could I squashed the overripe fruits against my body, rolled in them on the big table where they had been served. Then I looked up suddenly. At the door was a horde of ants, roaches, locusts, grasshoppers, and other unidentifiable insects racing toward me. I leaped from the table, slipped on fruit juice–slickened feet and fell. The bugs swarmed over me, their sour stench in my nostrils. I got up and started running— out the back door and then down a rocky path, slapping my skin to kill the gnawing bugs as I went.

The path hurt my bare soles but I kept moving as fast as I could go. Ahead of me was the light of day on a grassy, hilly coastline that I remembered from some forties film I'd seen on AMC. Behind me was the darkness of the hungry insect horde. The bugs on my skin cried out to the swarm, beckoning to them. I could hear their billions of scuttling feet and fluttering, buzzing, singing wings. The air was filled with the clicks and cries of bug life and its single-minded instinct to devour.

I was getting tired, very, very tired. Before me was a hill on top of which stood a cottage with yellow walls and a green and brown grass roof. The road didn't lead to the cottage and for some reason I felt that leaving the stony path would mean the beginning of the end. This phrase repeated in my mind over and over: the beginning of the end, the beginning of the end, the beginning of the end . . .

Finally I broke away and ran up the hill toward the cottage.

The swarm behind me let out a tremendous inhuman

victory cry. I fell to my knees, rose up, ran a few paces, fell again . . .

"Come on," she cried. "Hurry up."

A young black woman dressed like a peasant from eighteenth-century Europe stood at the open door gesturing toward me. I ran for her, falling and rising again and again, the insects gibbering and screeching at my back.

As soon as I got to her she grabbed my arm and pulled me inside. She slammed the door shut and then went around the room closing the shutters on the windows until the only light in the room came from an oil lantern set upon a rough-hewn table.

With a butter knife the young woman scraped the insects off my skin. Those that were still alive she crushed underfoot.

In the meantime I could hear the bug army gnawing at the walls and the roof. I could see their antennae waving under the door, trying to press their way in.

"Don't worry," the young woman said. "The roof grows forever and the walls have the whole earth between us and them."

Now she was washing the dead bugs and dried fruit juices from my skin with a tattered rag using water from a wooden bucket. She kissed the head of my penis and said something nasty before licking it.

I tried to back away but she grabbed the shaft of my rising erection and I went still.

She said something in a local dialect. It might have been English but I didn't understand. She stood up still holding my erection and took off her blouse and dress using only one hand. I was surprised because my dick stayed hard.

The trouble I always had with women was that I found it difficult to maintain an erection. Sometimes even during intercourse I'd lose the feeling.

But this time I was so hard that it ached. And the black peasant girl from the eighteenth century was naked, beautiful. She knelt down in front of me and stroked my erection gently with one finger and her thumb. It was maddening.

The insects were gnawing from all sides. They shrieked and squealed but I maintained my erection.

"I'm afraid," I said.

"Do you like this?" she asked.

"What?"

"The way I'm touching you."

"The bugs'll eat their way in."

"Come for me."

"The insects . . ."

"Come," she said and I did.

She held me as I bucked and grunted and while the insects pressed and cried. I couldn't stop the orgasm. It jittered inside me like a frantic insect trying to claw its way out.

The woman was still on her knees, still holding me.

"Should I let you go?" she asked. "Has this been enough?"

The walls were wavering as if they were made from paper. I could tell that the insects had eaten their way almost through to us. I wanted to be afraid but instead I could only think that the orgasm was meant to last moments and not minutes. This seemed very important. The throbbing passion in my body was crushing me, destroying me.

"Yes," I said as daylight began to show from the disintegrating walls and roof. "Let me go . . ."

At that moment my hand was repelled from the log as if

it were holding a high voltage line. I was thrown back in my chair.

The white orb at the center of the creature was open wide but it had migrated a few inches toward the breathing slit. We gazed at each other a moment and then it receded again.

It took me a few moments to realize that I had forgotten how to breathe.

I glanced at the clock in the kitchen. It was only 7:47, not even an hour since the standing branch had made its appearance. But in my mind many days had elapsed. It wasn't just the waking nightmare. It was also Frank and Pete, my father and Nicci, my mother who I barely remembered. I had gone over our relationships together from the beginning.

I had never in my life thought so deeply about anyone or anything.

The front of my pants had a dark damp spot from the wet dream–nightmare.

I took off my clothes and went to take a bath. I washed myself with soap and a hand rag for a long time, paying close attention to every part of me. It wasn't that I felt dirty but that I wanted to do a complete, a full job.

Usually I rushed through everything I did: eating, brushing my teeth, getting to work, leaving on time. I dressed quickly in the morning and thought about leaving the minute I got anywhere. If a movie was starting I'd look at my watch counting down the minutes until the credits began rolling and I could leave.

I even timed sex. How long could I last? How long was long enough?

But that evening in my porcelain-coated wrought-iron tub I washed my entire body with meticulous attention. My fingers and toes, the small of my back and the dead skin of my forearms—all scrubbed clean.

After the bath I toweled my feet and back, my legs until they were as dry as a desert.

After that I went in my bedroom closet and dressed. It was getting late and after my trancelike encounter with the vibrating log I was sure that I would go to sleep. But now I had on my black slacks and a white button-up shirt tucked in at the waist, cinched by a red leather belt. I put on socks and hard-soled shoes that I retied six times before they gave the proper snug fit.

Then I went to check on my beastly guest. It was breathing more easily now, hardly shaking at all. I wondered if I should call anyone. The super? The police? Pest control?

But I wasn't afraid of the thing. It might have been a monster but it hadn't tried to hurt me. It was a vegetarian. In the old days I would have tried to find some scientist or newspaper that would pay me for a look at that thing. But I didn't need money and I didn't want to be on the news.

I sat back at my table and turned to the first page of the first volume of *The Popular Educator Library*. I had read up through the seventh volume but it occurred to me in the bathtub that I couldn't explain anything that I'd read. I'd seen all the words, remembered the basic terms without understanding them, and then gone rushing ahead to the next topic, hurrying forward like I did with everything.

I turned to the first page of the first volume, the introduction, and read the words that editors rendered to explain,

excuse, or maybe to prepare me for the terrain that lay ahead.

I hadn't read the introduction up until then. I never read intros. I always thought that the main body of the book should explain the purpose and that prefaces and introductions were useless.

Not that I read many books that had introductions. And of the thousands of books I'd started I'd only finished maybe as many as a hundred . . .

THE TEN VOLUMES, which my father bought from a used bookseller in New Hampshire, were lovely. They were hardbacks with heavily textured deep maroon covers that had a golden crescent that arced through the series title.

I ran my fingers over the roughened cover and read the name over and over again. For some reason I looked at the clock then. It was 10:29. I had spent more time in the bathtub than I had with the wheezing log remembering the greater part of my personal history. There seemed to be something very important about this realization; that more time didn't necessarily give more experience. A tiny diamond held in a mountain of rock came to mind . . .

THE POPULAR EDUCATOR LIBRARY was originally written for the veterans returning from World War I, men who had given their school years to the war and were now starting families and didn't have time for a formal education. It was compiled by experts in the various fields of study and

meant to create a basis for a whole life of learning, just like real college is meant to be.

My father was in the room. He was wearing what he called his "medium blue suit" and his hair was combed and he had all his teeth. He was sober and stayed sitting next to me as I imagined a world that was gone but still managed to pass its knowledge along to me.

I began to reread the lectures on accounting: Double-entry bookkeeping with all its debits and credits and accounts that had to be balanced. I went over the articles again and again trying to understand the necessity for a zero balance. How could you have profit or debt if everything was equal?

I remember surprising myself by thinking that it was like the word "red." We called things red not because the word had any influence over the color but because we had to call it something. The words were made up just like dollar bills and ledgers. It was a mind game that we played.

I entertained this thought for a very long time. I might have spent days pondering but then I heard something.

"Food."

It was now a little after eight in the morning. I had spent the entire night reading and rereading about accounting. I understood most of what I had read and, like my bath, it me made feel complete if only for the moment.

I went to the log and found it slightly changed. The "eye" was open and there were swellings toward the middle and at the top of the breathing slit.

"I have to go down to the market to get more fruit," I said.

"Food."

I was already dressed and so I went into the hall and down the stairwell. I hadn't been outside in the commuter morning in months. Ever since winning the lottery I stayed in until late in the afternoon and then I only went out to eat at Milo's or to buy food from the corner market.

THE HO HO DELI was run by a family of Cambodians that had lived in New York for twenty-seven years. The man and wife were older and somber. They were short people and almost always together, their shoulders touching, their clothes nearly the same. The Thieus spoke poor English but over the years we had come to understand each other.

"Goddamn chinks wanna own all our shit," Pete used to say whenever we went into the small store together.

"They're from Cambodia," I once said, embarrassed by his loud insults.

"And where the fuck is that?" my rotund black friend asked.

"Next to Vietnam," I said. "My father was there in the war."

"And Vietnam is next to China and they got a billion people and they all chinks, every one of 'em."

The son, Bob Thieu, was in his twenties and friendly enough.

"Good morning, Mr. Redman," he said to me on the morning after I discovered the breathing branch. "I haven't seen you this early in a long time."

Bob knew that I had won the lotto; I'd bought the winning ticket from him. He never said anything about it

though. He made small talk with me and took my money. He was short like his parents, the color brown that bronze gets when it hasn't been polished for a long time. He kept his hair cut short and he had a Puerto Rican girlfriend named, or maybe nicknamed, Essa, whom his parents hated. Mr. and Mrs. Thieu both worked in the back of the store unless both Bob and his sister Nora were off.

The elder Cambodians rarely smiled and they were impatient with most customers. After five years of going there Mrs. Thieu would put a small piece of hard candy in the bag whenever I bought anything. I understood that this was her way of being friendly, of thanking me for patronizing their store.

"Yeah," I said to Bob as I put six prepackaged bags of six apples each on the counter. "I quit my filing job and now I usually sleep till noon."

"You making pie?" he asked.

"Yeah," I said. "Yeah. My sister is coming in from out west and she loves to bake."

Whenever he smiled Bob Thieu tilted his head to the side pointing his gaze toward the roof. There was something religious and vulnerable about his friendly grin.

"I never met your sister," he said.

I nodded not wanting to carry the lie too far.

"Did you hear about the monster, Mr. Redman?" Bob asked then.

"Say what?"

"On the television," he said, pointing to shelf behind him.

There nestled between the over-the-counter medications and cigarettes was a small black-and-white TV. The *Dr.*

Don Show was playing. A skinny black woman was on the chair next to the sympathetic-looking TV psychologist. In her hands she was holding the framed photo of a heavyset young black woman.

"What monster?"

"In Paris. They found it, it looked like a dead tree only it had these white teeth, fangs. They found it sucking a woman's blood in her apartment. When the police tried to grab it it swung around and killed one of them and then the other cops shot it."

I glanced back up at the television. Pasty white and corpulent, Dr. Don was now holding the woman's hands in one of his. With his other hand he gestured toward a curtain. The screen parted and the young woman from the photograph walked out. The older woman's mouth fell open and she jumped to her feet. The women embraced and even though I couldn't hear what was being said tears came to my eyes.

". . . and they found one in San Francisco," Bob Thieu was saying. "When the doctors tried to cut it open it let out a poison gas and twelve people got sick. Three of them died . . ."

He was handing me the change from the fifty I'd given him. I took my change and the apples and walked away, contemplating the connection between impossible reunions and deadly monsters.

THE ALIEN BEING had come down from the couch and was at the refrigerator, lying there lifelessly. I took out an apple and held it up to the long. The tubes shot out and sucked the

fruit down. It ate fifteen apples before slumping back into its satisfied comatose state.

After a few failed attempts at hefting the heavy thing I managed to carry it back to the couch and lay it out like a sleeping child. The upper portion of the creature, below the swollen top of the body, had flattened. And the white spot, the thing I thought of as an eye, had moved up to the center of this flat plane. My hand passed by the slit and a tube jutted out for an instant, piercing the skin before pulling back in.

Was this the beginning of the creature's taste for blood?

While the thing slept and wheezed I turned on the TV. There were monsters all over the news. In New Delhi, Johannesburg, Baghdad, and San Francisco. Branchlike beings that were deadly dangerous in every case. The news reporter, Kathy Long, said that there was no explanation for the origin of these beings. In each case they just appeared, seemingly out of nowhere and attacked.

Love Marin, the woman in San Francisco, said that she was studying the thing when it bit her. She claimed that it was making noises that she couldn't understand.

"It was trying to talk to you," I said to the TV screen. "It was hungry, asking you for an apple or banana."

Health officials were intending to study the remains of the creatures, all of which had died, but they deteriorated quickly and it was speculated by TV experts that it would be hard to tell even what kind of life-form they were.

"The government has put out a call to anyone who might have seen one of these creatures," Kathy Long's voice said over an artist's drawing that was only somewhat similar to the thing sleeping on my couch, "to report it to the CDC.

These things are dangerous. Seven people have already died from being in contact with them."

She went on and on describing the dangers the beings posed. They brought on experts, all of whom said they knew absolutely nothing about the creatures except that they seemed like some kind of improbable hybrid of plant and animal.

I sat there in my straight-back chair next to my own pet monster watching the news and wondering what I should do. I didn't feel that the thing posed a threat to me. He was just hungry or tired. He pierced my skin once but that was probably a mistake and I only bled a little.

As the afternoon went on more creatures were announced from around the globe. Tokyo, Manchester in England, and Milan all reported *monsters* that drank blood and shattered bones, emitted poisonous gasses, or cried out like banshees.

Now and then I'd regard my guest. Most often its white on white, blue-veined eye was staring back at me. It lay patiently resting; the creatures that they talked about on the news attacked their hosts within minutes of their first encounter.

I noticed that the creature's breathing slit was curving and the brownish fleshlike wood around it was gaining mass. The lower portion of the thing had a long line running down to the splayed root system at the bottom.

"A scientist in Mongolia," Kathy Long announced breathlessly, "has found and frozen a pole-snake in the Gobi Desert. Tuk Li Leung, a biologist from China originally, discovered one of the things in his hermetically sealed research laboratory. When he was asked how he thought the

pole-snake had found its way into the locked room he said that the only possibility is that it grew there."

The screen was showing a headshot of Long with a photograph of a dark-skinned Asian man above the left side of her head.

"Bill?" Long said, looking up toward a space behind me.

"Yes, Kathy?" a man's voice answered.

Suddenly an inset opened to the right of her head. In this was the streaming image of a tall black man in a short-sleeved shirt.

"Have you found out what actually happened in Professor Tuk's lab?" Long asked.

"He had been reading about this fabulous phenomenon over the Internet when he saw the thing standing upright right in front of him. He grabbed it and pushed it into large freezer used to keep specimens. I don't speak his language so we can only communicate through his translator but he seemed very excited."

"Could the thing we're calling the pole-snake have been developed in Tuk's lab?" Long asked.

"I don't think so, Kathy," Bill said. "These things have shown up in too many places that couldn't possibly have anything to do with this isolated area. But experts are coming in from all over the world to—"

I switched off the news at that point. They didn't have any idea about what they were saying. The creature that had appeared in my apartment was a delicate thing, a lost thing. It was hungry and shivering.

It was also transforming but peacefully—it seemed.

The government wanted to study it but what did I care about the government? They wanted my tax dollars to kill

Afghans and Iranians and all kinds of other people. Frank was right, I was no genius but I didn't need to be a brainiac to keep quiet and feed my pet his apples.

After all, I knew what it was like to be different.

I stuttered badly until the age of thirteen. That was the year the state took me away from my father and placed me in foster care. Kids made fun of me and adults got impatient when I tried to say anything.

The people who took me in were the Warrens. I liked them even though they were pretty cold. Mrs. Warren brought me to a woman named Giselle Anaras. Giselle was a speech pathologist. She had a delicate pale face and green eyes. Our first lesson was the word "candle."

"Candle," the pretty young Belgian said.

"Ca, ca, ca, can, ca, ca, candle," I said.

We were sitting next to each other on her red sofa. She placed both hands on mine and smiled.

"Ca, candle," I said.

"With the candle came the light," she said.

I'll remember that feeling of elation for all of my life. It was like her smile just blew away the stuttering. At first it only happened when I was alone with her. Then she started taking me to restaurants and movies, department stores to buy presents for the Warrens, and on the Staten Island Ferry. We talked to each other while other people stood around and then one day, at a diner, I asked the waitress for a ham sandwich with melted American cheese.

When those words came faultlessly from my lips I was astonished. I looked at Giselle and she smiled. It came to me that the one thing I was never able to say was how much I loved that young woman.

Sitting there, next to the Breathing Branch, I remembered every detail, every nuance of Giselle. She offered me cookies and grape drink that first day and didn't ask for a thank you. Whenever I began to stutter she'd put her hand on my forearm.

It came to me that Nicci looked a lot like Giselle. On our first date I got shy about something and Nicci put her hand out to me . . .

I looked down and saw that my hand was on the branch. The white-on-white eye was gazing at me. There was a vein of pale greenish blue color within the pale orb. It was pulsing gently.

I took my hand away and the supple brown being, which was transforming over the hours, shuddered.

I went to the table and gathered the rest of the apples in my arms and placed them on the flat upper portion of the creature.

"If you get hungry eat these," I said to the glistening, aqua-tinted eye. "I'm gonna go buy a dictionary. I'll be back."

ON THE STREET I felt as if people were watching me, studying my every move. I always felt that way when I have a secret but this was the worst I'd ever experienced, bordering on paranoia. Even when I had just won the lotto I hadn't been so wary. For that first month hundreds of people called me: cousins I hadn't heard from in years, Nicci, investment companies, companies that wanted to lend me money until the checks came in. My landlord wanted to sell me my apartment for a million dollars. Women whom I'd never met before asked me out on dates. I finally had to

turn the ringer off on my phone and only listen to the message service once a day.

But my problems hadn't stopped with the phone. People on the street recognized me, accosted me. One man, who I didn't remember but who said that we'd been in the third grade together, wanted me to come to his house so his wife could make us dinner. When I said no he wanted to fight, said that I was insulting him.

I got over those problems though. I bought a hat and grew a mustache, walked with my head down and went out mostly after dark. I didn't mind. It didn't matter much to me. All I cared about was that I didn't have to go to a goddamn job every day. People didn't correct me with sneers on their faces or turn away when I expressed any kind of idea. I was gliding through life on my own personal platinum sled and that was worth a few hands held out and scams laid out and people making up relationships that never were.

But that afternoon I was nervous. The branch appearing in my living room was more than the lotto. It was as famous as Muhammad Ali. People all over the world, governments, armies, and spies would be looking for it soon. And I was one of the few, maybe the only one, who knew where a living pole-snake was. And even though I knew that I should give it up I also knew that I would not.

The branch had come to me and asked me in single syllables to protect and feed it. It trusted me like a starving infant in a stranger's arms. It didn't break my bones or poison the air. It watched me and infused my dreams with some kind of crazy knowledge that let me know myself better than I ever had before.

Fuck the world and the governments, scientists, and

news anchors. They didn't care about me or the living branch or anything that mattered.

"I NEED A DICTIONARY, Mr. Slatkin," I said to the old white man who sat at the back desk of *Slatkin's Used Books and Such*.

"At a loss for words, eh, son?" the bespectacled old man said.

I'd been coming to his bookstore since I was five, back when he kept stacks of comic books in a corner next to the science fiction rack.

At a loss for words. It struck me that over the twenty-eight years I'd visited the old man he was trying to educate me with humor and a little twist in the language. This seemed very important at that moment.

"Something wrong, Rahl?" Mr. Slatkin asked me. "You seem kind of off."

"I am that, sir," I said. "I don't know most of the words and don't understand the few that I can say. I've been reading this book and a lot of what it says I have to guess at."

Slatkin scratched his jaw and stared at me. Then he smiled and stood up with a sigh.

"Getting old," he said.

"Getting better," I intoned.

He turned and looked at me again. This stare made me shy and so I picked up a book off his desk. *Bright Tomorrows: The Odyssey from Hobo to Architect* by Jared Simms. I flipped through a few pages but when I looked up Slatkin was still looking at me.

"Something wrong?" I asked the old man. His skin was

pale and festooned with liver spots. He wore suspenders
and a belt, a short-sleeved yellow shirt, and green pants that
had little shape and might have been older than me.

"My father used to say the same thing to my mother
when I was a boy not twelve blocks from this spot. She'd
feel a pain and say, 'Getting older,' and my father would
say, 'Getting better,' in Yiddish. But when you just said that
you sounded just like him. You . . ." He stared at me with
wonder or maybe even awe.

"It just came into my head, Mr. Slatkin. I didn't even
know I was sayin' it."

The older man stared at me a moment more. His scru-
tiny made me think about myself. My mind seemed to me
like an open field with mountains, forests, the desert, and
an endless plain on the four sides of me. I could go anywhere, do anything. The world was waiting for me and I
was waiting for a sign.

"Are you walking?" Slatkin asked.

"Yes, sir . . . that and the bus."

"Vell," he said. "I have an old dictionary. But it is hardback and must weigh twelve pounds . . ."

"Put it in a double bag, Mr. Slatkin," I said. "You know,
life's just a heavy weight on a long road anyway."

The old man, who had by this time hefted the big book
down from a shelf next him, dropped the tome and put his
hand to his heart.

"Papa?" he gasped. "Papa, is that you?"

"What's wrong, Mr. Slatkin?" I rushed to him, took his
arm.

"It vas even his voice," he said, amazement spreading
across his face.

"What was?"

"Vat you said. It vas my father talking to me. He had a cart in the East Village, right here. He vould sell old things and talk to me. Vhenever he had to carry something heavy he'd say . . ." Mr. Slatkin said something that was probably Yiddish, "and I vould laugh."

"I'm sorry, sir," I said. "I didn't mean to upset you. I didn't know what I was saying."

"But how could you know these things?" he asked. As he spoke his accent got deeper, more pronounced.

"I, I don't know. I was just talking."

He seemed to be standing all right on his own so I bent down and lifted the heavy book. The second edition of *Webster's New Twentieth Century Dictionary*. More than nine inches thick, over two thousand pages. I'd never owned a serious dictionary before.

"How much, Mr. Slatkin?"

"You can have it, Raleigh," he said. "You can have it."

"I can pay for it," I said.

"No. No. You already have paid me. You reminded me. You, you took me back to a time, a place . . ."

He held out his hand and we shook as if we had concluded a very important transaction. Then he fell back into his chair and stared up into space, a quizzical look in his eyes.

He hadn't given me a bag but I didn't want to bother him anymore. I was afraid to say something else like his father so I took my prize and walked out into the afternoon sun.

"Harry," I said out loud for no reason as I crossed the northern border of Cooper Union college. I knew somehow that this was Mr. Slatkin's first name. I tried to re-

member if he had ever mentioned his name but our talks were not personal in that way. I was always asking questions about war books or Doc Savage while he asked me about school.

I started feeling the dictionary's weight around then. After a while I stopped to sit on a bus stop bench. Sitting there in the Plexiglas shelter I experienced a kind of double image. The asphalt street in front of me became cobblestone and the people looked different, were dressed differently. A man pulling a cart passed by. His name, I knew, was Aaron, Aaron Slatkin, born in Estonia and immigrated to New York in 1904. He had a ragged salt-and-pepper beard and wore a heavy black coat even in the heat.

"You gettin' in or what?" a woman shouted.

I was standing, had one foot on the first step of a waiting bus. The large black woman bus driver was yelling at me. I hurried on, running my MTA card though the stripe reader as I went. I hustled to a seat and settled in with the big book on my lap.

Even through the hallucination I was moving forward in the real world. Real world. *What was real?* I wondered. Aaron Slatkin's memory was everything to his son Harry. My father, dead from drink, was the most important person I'd ever known.

Sitting there, disturbed over my visions and Mr. Slatkin's response to me I opened the book to the introduction and started reading.

The second edition was an important one it seemed. After World War II language had changed greatly and so the dictionary had to transform itself to fit what Americans were saying and reading. It was odd, I thought, that language

could change and that new words pushed out old ones. It occurred to me that if enough time went by people would be speaking English and I wouldn't understand a word they said.

"You gonna read that whole big book?" a young woman asked.

I'd been sitting next to her but hadn't noticed anything about her, distracted as I was.

"Uh, um, yeah. I guess I am."

"Dang."

She was pretty. A little heavy and cute, like young women can be. She was dark of skin like me with features that were rounded, reassuring.

I looked up and saw that the bus was coming to my stop.

"I have to get off here," I said.

"So?"

"It would have been nice to talk to you."

My response surprised her. I could see that she wanted to say something but couldn't find the words. I stood up and smiled at her.

When I got to the exit well at the front I looked back and she raised her hand making a tentative good-bye wave.

The bus driver growled at me saying something rude but I didn't understand what she said and didn't want to either.

I STOPPED AT THE THIEUS' MARKET and bought six more bags of fruit. Apples, mangoes, and pears. I lugged these up the stairs with my used dictionary and made it to my sun-starved but still brightly lit apartment.

The news monster's white eating tubes were consuming the second to last apple on its chest. It struck me then that the loglike creature had been transforming into a vaguely human shape. For some reason this didn't surprise me.

I sat myself down next to my new friend.

"You got a good appetite, Wood," I said giving the creature a name.

"Good," it said clearly, still in a child's voice.

"I brought you more."

"Enough now. Need no more. Sleep we will. Touch me."

From the top sides of the forming chest nubs had sprouted. These I understood would be Wood's arms. I placed two fingertips on a burgeoning limb. I felt a tingling followed by a shiver experienced by Wood but felt by me.

I WAS BLIND as a worm but I could feel the world around me with every cell of my being. Tactile sensations, radiations, scents, and something that I could only describe as differing auras of essence surrounded me. There was a thing in front of me that emitted a quality of great size and tranquillity.

"The ocean," I said in my mind.

"No," Wood said. "It is the void between your world and mine."

"But it isn't empty."

"It is full with a billion billion places like my home and your home. It is a place of many things and nothing."

All around me creatures were moving. They touched and sang, transformed into different physical bodies while staying the same inside, in essence.

"What is it that I'm, I'm knowing, seeing, feeling in my head?"

Wood laughed a child's laugh.

"You are feeling the world, its history and its intentions," the child's voice said. "If you concentrated your mind could follow the lines of being around this entire planet. You could see the Isle of the Mighty floating on a sea of molten rock or the cloud dwellers in their gaseous bodies dancing around the world. You could even experience the cold that grows in the south, the thing that is killing us by increments."

As Wood spoke I *saw* these things. There loomed a great island made of metal floating through molten lava in the center of the crater of a volcano that was at least fifty miles wide. I saw playful puffs of steam moving with intention miles above a red and yellow plane.

And then there was a place of gray withering; a cancer in a rough circle a hundred miles in diameter. All around the circumference life had fled. There was nothing near the perimeter of the tumor, not even plants or flies or whatever kind of life that existed on Wood's planet.

"My world is dying," Wood said, "the Giants and Wraiths and Walking Trees; the Mountains of Thought and the tiny Spores that guard us in our sleep."

Again as Wood's thoughts came into my mind I saw huge beings that blocked the sky walking past. I saw trees that glided through the soil with specks of light dancing around them lighting a purple night with trails of yellow glitter.

The glitter seemed to have a sound, a tinkling, a ringing. Something so crude as vibrations in the air didn't seem to fit in Wood's seamless world of mind and being.

I heard the sound again. This time I realized that it was the telephone. I could still feel the place that Wood was showing me but the call of the world made it fade in my mind. I moved my hand away and both Wood and I shuddered violently.

"HELLO?" USUALLY I WOULD HAVE let the machine pick up but I wasn't thinking and so I answered the call.

"Hi, honey," Nicci said.

She seemed a long way away and far in the past. I couldn't remember what she looked like or what feeling had passed between us.

"Oh," I said. "Hey."

"Hey? That's all you have to say?"

"Um, I don't know. I was doing something."

"You said you were going to call me."

I didn't remember but Nicci wouldn't lie about that.

"I got, uh, busy," I said.

"With who?" Nicci said jealous of the man she had cuckolded and left.

"I . . ., I'm just here reading and . . . thinking about things."

"That sounds really boring," she said. "Let me come over and we can do something fun."

"I can't."

"Why not? Is there someone there with you?"

"It's a guy," I said. "John, John Wood. I used to know him in high school and I ran into him in the street. He was homeless you know and so I'm letting him sleep on my couch for a couple'a days."

"Well," Nicci reasoned, "if it's a guy then he won't mind if you take me to dinner."

"Sure," I said, feeling the excruciating ecstasy of giants striding through my mind.

They were like huge sculptures of six-legged rams moving slowly through great fields of scarlet fungus that grew a foot an hour and would cover the whole planet in a year if not for the grazing of the gargantuan herd.

"So you'll be there?" Nicci asked.

"What's the address again?" I asked.

"Si Fan at the Hall-Foreman Building," she said. "Seventy-sixth floor."

"At six?"

"At eight," Nicci said. "Aren't you listening to me, Rahl?"

"Eight o'clock at Si Fan," I said. "I'll even wear that suit you made me buy before you started fucking Tom Beam."

I hung up before she could complain. It was cruel of me to say that but I didn't know how to stop myself. Wood's presence in my mind had knocked my civility for a loop.

I went back to the manikin and sat down. The nub growing from the slowly forming shoulder moved, reaching out to me.

"Can you speak?" I asked.

"Yes."

"Then let's talk for a while," I said. "I need to get over all that shit you showed me."

"I and one, two, three, four, five, six, seven, eight, nine, ten, eleven of my comrades from our world were bundled into forms like this thing you see before you and sent across the void to this place . . . Earth."

I noticed that the slit Wood breathed through was now

nearly horizontal, like a human mouth. The voice was still that of a child's but different somehow.

"So you are twelve people?" I asked.

"No. We are each a bundle sent to your world to make contact."

"Why?"

"The growing cold," Wood said and again a shudder went through us both.

"You have to escape before it kills everything," I said.

"Yes."

"And you are coming to Earth."

"We have sent millions of our peoples bundled into growing blocks into the void," Wood said. "Giants and Cloudlings, Walking Trees and Razor Men, Mountains of Thought and . . ."

For a very long time Wood listed the kinds of life that were bundled and sent off into the portal between worlds. Once or twice I tried to interrupt but the creature either did not hear me or actually couldn't stop once it started.

". . . Flower Children and Stone Bearers, Mists of Light and even the Calm of Darkness have banded and bundled and gone off in search of homes for our peoples," Wood said finally going silent.

"You're a real chatterbox, Wood," I said.

"What is that?"

"Somebody who just keeps on talking and talking and can't stop."

"Where I come from," the high voice replied, "all questions are answered in their entirety. Nothing is left to consider. If you touched me I could pass everything in an instant."

"But I lose myself when we touch," I said noticing a swelling in the manikin's chest. The eye was now above the mouth and it seemed to be splitting like the zygotes we studied in biology at school.

"You aren't used to me yet," Wood said. "Soon you will be able to dance in my mind as I do in yours."

The prospect of an even deeper relationship with the alien being frightened me. As it was I had never been so intimate with anyone. I felt Wood in my mind on the street. I was sure that the presence of this extraterrestrial in me read the emanations from Mr. Slatkin's mind.

"You say that all the different life-forms on your planet are looking for homes?" I asked, maintaining my distance by continuing to keep our communication on a verbal level.

"Only one intelligent life-form exists where I am from," Wood said. "That is the only life."

"Even the red fungus?" I asked.

At that moment Wood's eye split in two.

"Yes. The fungus grows on the back of the Yellow Bone Women who sleep for centuries waking now and then to climb the Mountains of Desire. The Giants eat away the fungus to protect the yellow specters from being crushed and the world from suffocating on their wastes . . ."

Wood described how the Bone Women slept under certain stone formations so that the giant six-legged ram-things would not crush them as they grazed. The alien went on to explain how the Mountains of Desire held the passions of every being on the planet. They filtered love and hate and community. This sent Wood off on a long description of how decisions were made on a planetwide basis for all the life-beings (as he called them) everywhere.

Even in their sleep the Yellow Bone Women participated through their dreams.

Wood lectured me for two hours or more. I was overwhelmed and confused by what I learned but I couldn't stop listening any more than Wood could stop talking. When it finished I wanted to get up and leave but I still had a question.

"But what does it mean, Chatterbox?" I asked. "Are the Mountains of Thought and Spores of light related?"

"We are all the same life-form cast into different roles," the child's voice informed me.

A spore could mate with a mountain on Wood's planet and together they might spawn a tree. This was obvious and needed no further explanation.

"I have to go," I said. "I'm supposed to go see a woman I know."

"Woman? Like the Bone Women?"

"No. On this planet all the life-forms are related but cannot mate between the species. Animals have a male and a female and only they can make more of that particular species."

"You cannot grow apples with your body?"

"No."

"Curious."

I brought all the fruit from the Ho Ho Deli and placed it around the being I called Chatterbox and Wood.

"I don't know how long I'll be gone."

"I shall save myself for your return," the child's voice vowed.

The notion of the promise disturbed me but I couldn't say why.

WHEN I GOT OUTSIDE my building I realized that it was only six thirty. I had an hour and a half to kill and so decided to walk up to Fifty-ninth Street where the restaurant was located. On the way I thought about what it meant to harbor an alien who admitted that his race wanted to inhabit our planet. I hadn't discussed the news items about his fellow travelers because I was afraid of Wood's reaction to the barbaric treatment that my race had given his. I wanted to know more. I wanted to show the bundle of transformation that some of us were friendly.

Once again I considered turning Wood in to the authorities. Maybe that way I could be a kind of a translator for the alien world. But I didn't trust humanity very much. I never had a real friend or a parent I could rely upon. No one complained when I graduated high school and became a file clerk. I had twenty-six million dollars coming to me but that was just a fluke; I hadn't earned, deserved, or even stolen the money. I wasn't in any real sense a part of the world.

One touch of Wood's alien skin and I was closer to his reality than I had ever been to my own.

The skyscrapers and boulevards of Manhattan paled in comparison to the crystalline Mountains of Desire with their milk-white waterfalls and blood-red rivers. The crowds of people on the street seemed like lonely motes of single-cell lives drifting aimlessly on a microscope's slide. They didn't know how minds could merge and reemerge as part of a whole.

I passed a white woman at Thirty-ninth and Broadway who wore a silver dress and red high heels. In human terms

she was lovely but sad. Her mind was on a man, an old man who lay dying in a room that was barred to her. He was surrounded by old women and grown children who did not love him. His labored breath sounded in my ears as it did in hers. I could see that in his mind he was thinking of the silver-clad white woman—Cora. He worried how she would survive without him and felt jealousy that she'd have to find another man to pay for her. And she was worried about him, about how lonely he'd be. Yes, she'd find another man, she already had, was on her way to meet him even then, but she loved Milford because he talked to her and looked her in the eye when she spoke.

I found myself following Cora at a distance. My mind leaped from place to place until it alit on a man who called himself Gone. His real name was Philip and he was going to work at St. Christopher's at that moment. Gone was a black man like me. He had done many things in his life. He'd lost heart like Milford, who lay dying, and he was desperate, like Cora who lived by her beauty and also suffered from it.

I saw all this as clearly as if it were a story being told to me by my mother before the lights were turned off.

"Excuse me," I said to the young woman. "Cora?"

"Do I know you?" she asked.

I was wearing my charcoal-colored suit. I looked presentable so she stopped.

"There's a guy, a practical nurse named Philip Rune who calls himself Gone," I said.

"So?" Cora said. She began to edge away.

"He works at the hospital Milford is in," I said and she stopped.

"How do you know about Milford?"

"There's a man at the hospital that calls himself Gone," I said again. "He needs money. If you give him a hundred dollars he'll take you up to your boyfriend's room after the hospital closes to the public. He knows the schedules and so you can stay for a while every night until . . . you know."

"I don't have that kind of money," Cora said.

I took five hundred-dollar bills from my pocket and handed them to her. I still remember, even after all the terrible things that have happened to me, that her fingers were cold.

"This is all you'll need," I said and she started crying. It was a whimper at first and then it escalated into howling despair.

I put my arms around her and she cried and cried. People on the street glanced at us, some of them stopped and stared wondering if I was somehow hurting her.

After a few minutes she stopped crying and pulled away from the embrace.

"Who are you?" she asked.

"Nobody."

"Are you a friend of Milford's? Did he send you?"

"No. I was recently given a gift and now I'm paying it back."

I walked away from her, my mind moving around outside of my body like a restless dust devil down an empty and abandoned street.

"HAVE YOU BEEN WATCHING the news stories on those things?" Nicci asked.

We were sitting at a window table seventy-six floors above Central Park. The void of the park in the night reminded me of the Gulf Between Worlds Wood the Chatterbox had shown me. For a moment I could feel the alien thinking about me. Wood was wondering about my mother, about the notion of *mother*.

"Only a little bit," I said. "I've been reading a lot and taking care of John Wood."

"Why would you take some drug addict bum to stay in your house?" Nicci asked.

She was wearing pink silk, wearing it well. It hugged her porcelain cleavage and rode high on her shapely legs. Her pink shoes were semitransparent and the pale ruby in the ring on her right index finger seemed as if it were glowing from an inner light.

"I don't know," I said. "I guess I felt that sometimes you have to do something that doesn't make sense outside your own mind."

"Well," Nicci said, somehow dismissing my words, "you should watch about those pole-snakes. The one in Mongolia blew up."

"What?"

"It started growing insect arms and feelers," Nicci said with vehemence, "and then it got this big ugly head. It was getting bigger and bigger even though nobody was feeding it and then, when the scientists tried to keep it from breaking out it blew up."

"Are you ready to order?" an Asian man dressed in all black asked.

"I'll take the Porterhouse," I said. "Do you have brussels sprouts?"

"I'll ask in the back, sir."

Nicci ordered cod with horseradish potatoes and broccoli rabe. She also asked for another Manhattan. I wasn't drinking.

"How bad was the explosion?" I asked when the waiter went away.

"Fifteen hundred meters in circumference," she said obviously parroting some TV report, "and it left a crater thirty feet deep. Six hundred people died. The black reporter who works for CNN was killed."

"How many, how many of those things have they found?" I asked.

"Eight," Nicci said, happy to be able to tell me things I didn't know.

She went on for a while explaining how scientists around the world were baffled by the *pole-snakes* and their varied morphing, explosive, blood-sucking, and poisonous abilities. There were many camps of hypothesis about the creatures. One school of thought was that they were a life-form that lived deep in the earth and were being forced to the surface by mining, nuclear testing, and other ecologically irresponsible human acts. Others thought that Wood and his friends had come from another planet from this or some nearby solar system. Some scientists believed, because of the wide range of phenomena the creatures were able to manifest, that they were a life-form that had come into being in outer space and had come to Earth pulled by our gravity out of their natural habitat.

But the wildest, and most prevalent, belief was that these beings were angels sent by any of the many religious pantheons and that the end of the world was coming. The final

judgment was upon us, many everyday people believed, and these living poles were syllables in God's final verdict just as Moses's staff stood for his righteous rage three thousand years ago.

"Can I come home with you?" Nicci asked when we were standing outside waiting for a cab.

The offer caught me off guard. I wanted her. I even needed her. But I didn't trust her motives. I hadn't been able to read her mind; that wasn't something I could do consciously. Rather than invading Cora's thoughts I had been pulled into them.

I couldn't read Nicci's mind but I thought I knew what she wanted. I was a man with a lot of money and she wanted life to be easier. I could take her to Paris or Cairo, Tokyo and Hong Kong. And she could take my jittering restlessness and take it into a height that only she ever brought me to.

My sex life had been substandard at best. The girls and women I'd known lost interest in week or a night. I couldn't kiss right and it was very difficult for me to maintain an erection, especially in the condom-coated world of safe sex.

Nicci was the only girlfriend I ever had for more than a few weeks and sex with her was always good—at least for me. That's one of the reasons I was so sad when she left. As far as I was concerned she had taken my manhood along with her.

"Are you still mad about Tom Beam?" Nicci asked.

I realized that I had been standing there silently. She thought that this silence was my answer.

"Are you guys getting in?" a cabbie said from his window.

He'd stopped and I hadn't noticed.

"No," I said, waving him on. "No. We have to . . . have to talk."

"Fuck me," the driver said and gunned his motor. The tires squealed and a man walking near us jumped from fright.

The anger, violence, and fear all at once seemed to contradict or maybe mock the internal mechanism of Wood's mind; like three words pronounced in solitary articulation instead of being combined to make a statement.

"What's wrong, Rahl?" Nicci asked me. "Don't you like me anymore?"

"Sure I do, Nicci."

"You used to say that I was the only woman who made you feel like a man."

"You are."

"Then what?"

She had a beautiful face. And she knew how to look at you with both longing and gravity.

"You," I said and stalled.

"What?"

"I mean . . . I've been thinking about you, Nicci."

"I've been thinking about you too, Raleigh." She took my hand, smiling coyly.

"There was that guy, Morley something," I said.

The smile went away.

"Tambor," she said, releasing my hand.

"Yeah. After you left me I just sat in my house for three weeks. I would have been fired except my friend Frank got a nurse to steal a doctor's letterhead and he wrote me a note . . . said I had some virus that he looked up. Inner ear something that kept you from working for up to a month.

"All I did was think about you. I wanted you to come

back. I called you but your phone was disconnected. I went
to your place but you were never there. Tom Beam wasn't
listed so I went through all my old phone bills thinking that
maybe you called him. I went all the way back six months
and I found a strange number that had been called over
thirty times."

"It was just a thing, Rahl."

"I know that. I found three men's numbers other than
Morley's. The thing is you were the only girl's number I had
on those bills. You had more boyfriends than I had girl-
friends on my own bill."

"That's not my fault," she said.

Looking back on that period (what later came to be
known as "Before Ascension," B.A.) this was the only moment that the alien creature was not on my mind.

"I went to talk to Pete," I said.

"Because I went out with him?" Nicci asked.

It was the last time that she would hurt me but the feeling was exquisite, like a jagged knife plunged again and
again into a heart that just wouldn't die.

"No. I didn't know you went out with him too."

"Oh."

"No," I said again. "I went to Pete to get a gun."

It was the first time I had ever seen fear in Nicci's eyes.
She was a tough Italian girl born in Brooklyn and raised on
Staten Island. She knew mobsters' children and pub thugs
that beat blacks and Puerto Ricans for fun.

"You were gonna shoot me, Rahl?"

"I don't know," I said. "I was gonna to do somethin'.
You or me or Tom Beam, maybe Morley Tambor. But Pete
talked me out of it. He told me that he'd get the gun but he

wanted me to think about it first. I called him every day for a week and he'd tell me he was getting me a forty-five but he never did. I used to think he was doin' me a favor."

"Okay, Raleigh," Nicci said. "You win. I'll go."

She walked to the curb and raised her lovely hand. A taxi pulled right up, she got in, and was gone.

I stood out on the sidewalk for a long while. It was late but there were people out still; coming home from work, from dinner, from visits with the wives and husbands of their friends.

Wood came to mind then. In his world everyone was connected in deep and meaningful ways. No one was ever alone or wanted to be. No one owned or claimed property. I wasn't sure how I knew all that but I was certain about it. And though the notion of merging with everything soothed me I was still a human being living in isolation, looking at a world that I could barely touch and that I would never understand.

After a while I went to a payphone and dialed a number I'd known by heart since the age of nine.

"Hello?" he said on the first ring.

Pete still lived in his old room in the apartment with his mother. His father had died and his siblings, Esther and Duke, were off in the world. But Pete hung in there.

"Why didn't you tell me about you and Nicci?" I said.

"Because you an' her was still goin' out," he said, and I hung up—violently. The phone broke in half in my hand.

I WALKED HOME from Midtown trying to rebuild myself with steps like little bricks meant to make a wall between

me and what I was leaving behind. But I couldn't hide and I couldn't get away. I was thinking obsessively about Nicci, making love to her while even then she was seeing Morley and Pete and who knew how many others.

I tried to think a way around the humiliation but nothing I had was proof against what I'd lost. I felt like a leper dropping digits and limbs as I made my way toward oblivion. My mother, my father, my girlfriend, my manhood . . .

When I came into the apartment I had all but forgotten about Wood. But then I turned on the light and saw the manikin shifting on the sofa. At least I had someone (something) that depended on me. At least I had that.

Wood was pretty much the same: a half-formed doll shaped from smooth hard wood. The eyes were a little farther apart and the area around the breathing slit had thickened as if becoming lips.

I reached out, laying my hand on the nub of a shoulder. It might have seemed like a gesture of friendship but what I really wanted was to be pulled away into the whirlpool of Wood's alien world, dragged off by Yellow Bone Women into trees who in their dreams mapped the stars.

I expected the psychedelic experience of before but instead I found myself deep inside my own mind. I was shooting Pete and at the same time making fabulous love with Nicci on the sidewalk in front of the Hall-Foreman Building. My sexuality flooded her with reciprocal passion while Pete was running and I was shooting him with my gun, hitting him in the shoulder blade, the calf, his left hand. Across the street I stood straight and tall giving a lecture on the French and Indian Wars. I was fucking and shooting and orating all at once.

There was a feeling of elation coming off me, a rippling energy that escalated over the seconds. Blood flowed from Pete's wounds, a crowd gathered to hear my speech, and I was pounding away at Nicci on the verge of an explosive orgasm. And then, just as Pete died and the audience cheered, just as Nicci and I were coming, suddenly it was if my mind, my brain itself were sucked right out of me and into Wood.

The feeling was agonizing but there were also aspects, glimmers of pleasure. It felt as if everything I was had been flattened out onto a great plane of a slide under a huge microscope through which an intense light shone, illuminating every moment of my existence. My entire life was there, my first Monopoly game, my mother's breast, her face just beyond it, thick lips cooing as I sucked and bit at her hungrily. Mr. Montcalm was sitting at his desk in my eleventh-grade English class telling me that I was very smart and that I could get through college and make something of myself. I was wiping my ass in the third-floor boys' toilet of my elementary school thinking that I'd never get it clean enough. I was walking down Broadway behind three girls with thick Brooklyn accents wishing and fantasizing that they were talking to me.

I was trying to make love to Anetta Brown but couldn't stay hard. I was fighting with a boy named Arnold. I woke up in the middle of the night, thirteen years old, having just wet my bed—again.

The visions, memories, and feelings stood on line but in no particular temporal order. Some visions blended. My father came home drunk and got me out of bed. He started lecturing me about getting a good education and then he

was my mother saying the same words in the same voice. Pete was with Nicci. They were under the covers of my childhood bed. But then Pete was Frank and Nicci smiled at me. She threw the covers back revealing Frank's enormous rock-hard erection.

I witnessed these snippets of memory and imagination without emotional response. These were merely details that made up something larger than I could see. It came to me that the story of my life would take thousands of years to report in full. There were so many facts and factors, elements and details, perceptions both conscious and unconscious. And they were dull, monotonous; feelings without connection, actions without purpose.

An image stuck for a long while. I was seven years old, standing in the dressing room of a theater, staring at myself in a stained mirror. I looked into my eyes and features amazed that this was me. There was nothing now but this image. I didn't stutter because I wasn't talking. My father wasn't drunk because he wasn't there. I wasn't motherless because there was no question of mother in the room or the room in the mirror. Pete and Frank didn't matter because I had not met them yet.

That's when the pain ripped through me. It was as if someone had yanked the blood vessels right out of my arms and legs and chest. It hurt so much that I doubled over in my chair releasing Wood.

I screamed and fell from the chair. I couldn't open my eyes or think about anything but the pain. My muscles constricted and my fists tightened.

"Stand up," she said.

Stand up? I couldn't even breathe.

"Stand up, Rahl."

Who was talking? Was I still in the dream under the microscope?

I lifted my head and saw a copper-skinned woman with light brown eyes looking down on me. She was naked and young and supple. Her pubic hair stood out and I could see the outline of her vaginal lips. She held her hands out to me.

"Stand up," she said again.

The pain was gone. I stood, taking her hands as I did so.

"Wood?"

"My name is Cylla," she said.

Cylla, my make-believe girlfriend's name plucked from somewhere on that vast landscape under the microscopic plane.

"I am yours and you are mine," she said.

"But . . ."

"Take off your clothes, Rahl, we're going to make up for lost time."

Smiling, she started with the buttons of my shirt. I opened my mouth in protest. I might have even said a word or two but she leaned toward me and we kissed. It was the kiss I dreamed about as a child and later as a man. I wasn't off the mark, not at all, I was sure of myself but there was also something appropriately hungry and a little bit awkward about that kiss. It felt, I always knew it could feel like jumping into a lake for the first time that year. My neck moved left and then right working down into her mouth and she was smiling somehow while running the tip of her tongue between my gums and lips.

My pants fell down and she squatted down before me . . . I was on top of her, the vinyl sofa making little crying sounds

like the basketful of newborn kittens in Mrs. Brannert's apartment across the hall . . . "Don't come," Cylla said looking up into my eyes . . . A moment later I came and she did too laughing and squirming and calling out my name.

I was drunk on something. Maybe it was the experience of being examined so closely. Maybe it was from the excitement of having no fear of making love. We went into my bedroom and rutted on the floor.

She whispered things to me that I had always wanted to hear from a woman's lips at my ear; things that I could never repeat, not even in this confession.

When I couldn't make love anymore we kissed and murmured, touched and gazed.

"I don't understand," I said finally when we were nodding in the bed, almost asleep.

"I am the woman you have wanted, am I not?" she asked.

"I never dreamed of a woman like you."

"And yet you created me with your sadness and your lust," Cylla said.

"Why are you talking like that?" I asked.

She ran the baby finger of her left hand along the underside of my penis and it was erect again.

"I come from you, Raleigh," she said. "I came to you."

We were facing each other, lying on our sides. My heart skipped as I beheld her light-colored eyes and copper skin, which was almost metallic and yet warm and giving.

Her fingers closed lightly around my erection.

"Don't," I said, and her grip tightened.

That was what I wanted. Realizing this I said, "You do come from me," and she smiled. It was a smile I had known from as long ago as I could remember.

"What are you doing to me?" I asked.

"I haven't done anything yet."

She got up on her hands and knees with her back to me.

"Come on, Rahl," she said. "Come inside me."

I looked closely at her then. She wasn't a supermodel beauty, no. Many a man might pass her on the street with hardly a second glance. But this was the body and mind of the woman I longed for. It wasn't her pretty face but the way her eyes took me in. It wasn't the perfect skin but the way every touch was a stroke of love. Her eyes were wider apart than the norm. Her hair was a golden brown, thick and pushed back . . .

"No," I said.

"Why not?"

"Because I've never said it before. Because I never imagined saying no before."

Cylla smiled and curled down in front of me. I kissed her and it was the same as our first kiss.

"You want me," she said and I wanted her to say.

"I'm afraid of you," I said.

Cylla's face got serious for the first time in her short life.

"I know," she said. "You could be left alone without me."

"If I stay with you for even just one day I'd die if you ever left."

"I won't leave."

"Everybody says that."

"I'm yours," Cylla said.

I was about to say that she was not but I couldn't. Cylla *was* mine, she came out of me like Athena from Zeus, like Eve from Adam.

I gawped at her and she smiled. I was sweating, aroused, my heart was thumping and my fingertips tingled.

"It's like a fever, your love," Cylla said placing the flat of her hand on my forehead.

She was right. I tried to tell her so but the tears stopped me.

"We are the same," Cylla said with conviction. Her light eyes were luminescent, like fog lamps coming from far away down some unfamiliar road.

"You may have come from me," I said. "But you're perfect and I am anything but that."

"You saved me," she replied. "While eight of my fellow travelers were destroyed you fed me apples and pears."

"You know about them?"

"I know everything you know and, and also." She hesitated a moment, looking away from me. "And also I was connected to them. I felt them perish."

My erection had withered.

"What do you want, Cylla?" I marveled that her name came off my tongue so easily.

"To merge with you, Rahl."

"How could we be any closer?"

"We could be one," she said.

This last syllable was like a dark musical note, a warning, a dreadful tone. I wanted to take this further step with her but somehow I knew that word was a border and that if I crossed it there could be no return.

"You don't have to ask me do you?" I said.

"I could make you one with me but not without your asking for it."

"Why?"

"Because where I'm from it is easy to merge. It's like breathing. Any life-form on my planet could delve into any-one else regardless of what the other desires. But the Yellow Bone Women need solitude for their hibernations and the all-seeing eyes need darkness for contemplation. We each have special needs and so etiquette demands at least one party from that species agree to the invasion of instinct and knowledge, thought and dream. I would never bond with you without your agreement."

"There's more to it," I said.

Cylla smiled and touched my face.

"Yes."

I wanted to breathe. I wanted to get up and run. I was already in love with a woman who wasn't woman at all. She could have been a man or a whale or a monarch butterfly. Not that it mattered to me. I knew her so well that I could count her dreams in the night. But there was something more going on, something larger than I could understand.

"Don't tell me," I said.

"I have to."

"I don't wanna know. I just wanna, wanna love you like a man and a woman for a little while."

Cylla smiled and laid back on the bed.

"Shall we watch the news?" she asked.

She picked up the remote and pressed its buttons as if she had used it before. She knew the CNN number and en-tered it. They were talking about Afghanistan and how no foreign invader had kept that fiercely independent people down for long. She switched to FOX News where a blond

young man who looked somewhat like a football player was talking about an explosion in Moscow.

". . . four city blocks were leveled and there were deaths reported as far as a mile from the epicenter of the explosion," the newscaster said. "All public officials will tell us is that they don't know what caused the explosion, which seemed to be centered around a private research facility."

The image of a harried man in uniform appeared. He wore a toupee of short black hair and sported a salt-and-pepper mustache that was quite thick. He spoke in Russian but the volume of his speech was lowered and a woman's voice was used to translate his words.

"We do not know what has happened," he-she said. "No terrorism seems to be involved but how can we tell? The world is so crazy today. We will examine the source of the explosion . . ."

At that moment the scene on the TV screen changed. Now we were given an aerial view of an incredibly large crater in the middle of a big city. There were gouts of fire flaring up from broken underground gas mains. Here and there at the edges of the crater were piles of bodies.

". . . and find out what was its cause," continued the translator for the man in the incongruous wig. "We will find the source and if anyone is to blame they will be brought to justice."

"It was Racer who died," Cylla said softly.

"One of yours?"

"They wanted to experiment on her," Cylla said, though I wasn't sure that she was answering my question as much as talking to herself. "They fed her chemicals and exposed

her to many different life-forms. But it was too fast and her body went crazy. That's what you call it isn't it, Rahl? You are crazy when you no longer can make sense out of the world and you."

I nodded.

"And when we go crazy in bundle form," she continued, "we have to be absorbed or we explode."

"Could you have gone crazy?" I asked, worried and yet unwilling to run.

"Yes. But you fed my body and my part of the Great Soul. You gave me form and vision. You shared yourself with me: blood and spirit."

"You took my blood when you bit me," I said, "to study me?"

"To take your seed. To know the structure of your be-ing."

"Authorities in the States today," the blond-haired foot-baller said on returning to the screen, "have revealed that they believe the explosion in Russia is similar to the one in Mongolia the day before yesterday. It has been postulated that Russian scientists had in their possession one of the beings referred to as 'pole-snakes.' "

The TV image shifted again presenting a devious-looking man who was young, bald, white, and quite thin.

"American security scientists have discovered," the un-trustworthy man said, "using satellite surveillance that in every place on the globe where these creatures have appeared a unique radiation was emitted."

An image of the globe, flattened out like it is in some ge-ography books, took over the screen. In each of the places

that the pole-snakes had appeared a faint blue radiance was in evidence. There was one over New York City.

"The radiation," the thin reporter continued, "is of unknown origin. Specialists at the state department say that they only noticed the irregularity but have not been able to define its structure or source. But it is clear that wherever the radiation appears so have these deadly creatures . . ."

Again the flattened map appeared but this time the blue radiance was replaced with small black Xs. I noticed that there was one X in the middle of the Pacific Ocean and another in Brazil that had not been reported. There was also one over the African nation of Mali.

"These marks on the map," the now disembodied reporter said, "reveal the general area but not the exact locations of the sources of . . ."

"That one is us," Cylla said pointing at the screen. "They will be looking for me here."

My mind slipped away from Cylla at that moment. I was back inside the home college course my father had bequeathed. I remembered the concept of the period and the paragraph break. *The period ends a succinct element of an argument or thought and a paragraph either begins a new thought or continues an argument both related and yet somehow removed from what has gone before.*

Cylla pointing at the screen was the end of a very long and tedious paragraph of my life, a rambling run-on sentence. The next step, I knew, would be a new phase at the beginning of a new chapter.

"Let's go," I said.

"Go where?"

"I have my father's car in a garage on Ninety-second Street. We can get in it and get out of here."

Cylla knew everything about my life from the moment I was born, from the point at which my species began. But I knew her hardly at all. When I'd look into her face I tried to tell myself that she was an alien invader but all I could see was a woman that I loved but did not understand.

She pondered my offer.

"The man in the box says that they cannot pinpoint exactly where the radiance ends up," she said slowly.

"It comes from right here," I argued, touching her thigh.

"No, Rahl," she said like an old friend who had known me for years. "The radiation originates far up in the atmosphere. We all first appeared in the sky as glass wings that fluttered down to Earth. That was to avoid appearing within some solid form that would trap our bodies holding them motionless until we died."

"So you appeared in the sky but you were invisible?"

"Yes," she said in the way she had spoken when she was nothing but a tree branch with a vertical slit for a mouth.

"So they can't find us?"

"The radiant energy that brought us here was potent but it dissipated quickly. They will not find this house. They will not notice me."

I was staring at her, wondering what the thrumming feeling was in my mind and body. She was gorgeous to me. Her eyes had seen every corner of my tedious humdrum existence. She'd seen my fears and obsessions, my crush on Theda Brown in the sixth grade.

"What are you thinking?" Cylla asked.

"What's your last name?"

For a moment she was surprised, and her eyes grew wide, more beautiful. They shone like a golden idol's eyes in some primitive world where everyone belonged to each other.

"Bene," she said in the Italian form. "Cylla Bene. Your lover."

"Okay," I said. "Miss Bene. The world has changed in this room. What do we do now?"

"Shall we make love again? I like it when you kiss me down there."

"No, Cylla. What are your plans for my world, my people?"

"Immigrants from my world need to merge with yours," she said. "We are dying on my planet. We must leave and find new homes."

It was like watching a science fiction movie from the fifties, *The Blob* or *Night of the Living Dead,* only the monster was a beautiful woman who knew me and loved me.

"You want to merge with humanity?"

"Hardly," she said with a show of haughtiness that did not come from me. Or maybe it did.

"When we first perceived your world," she was saying, "we believed that the human race would be the prime factor in our transferal. But we were wrong. Your race is fearful and cruel. Now we have found others and only you, Raleigh Rexford Redman, among all humanity has accepted us and sheltered us and therefore you are the only human we can trust. You are the Prime One among humans."

"What others?" I asked. "There is no other dominant life-form on our planet."

"You are wrong, my love," she said. She stroked my cheek and the thrumming got stronger. "There are beings whose

intelligence rivals the hairless apes. And intelligence in the mechanical sense is not the only definition of colony or culture."

"Who are you talking about?"

Cylla placed three fingers of her left hand between her upstanding breasts.

"The answers to everything are inside of me," she said. "Say the word and we shall merge. We will become each other and you will know everything."

The vibration in my body turned to trembling. My hands shook, my teeth chattered. Cylla reached out and took my hands, she kissed my mouth.

"It's okay," she said. "You have time. No matter what happens you will survive the transition."

I could feel her breath on my chin and chest. She was human and she loved me more than even a mother could love her son or a child his mother. I had created the form that Cylla took. I was the mud and muck from which she arose.

But she was telling me something. She was always telling me something. There was a world beyond the world of my people. It was organizing even as we spoke—arming, preparing for a war that we could not win.

"What good is my survival if everyone else is dead?" I asked.

"You and I will survive together. We will make children. We will rebuild the world of man alongside the peoples of Ido."

"Ido?"

"That is the name given for the merging of your world and mine."

She sat there patiently looking at me. She was predicting the fall of the human race and I loved her, was afraid of her, and realizing through those emotions that I had to negotiate with her for the safety of my people.

"And you want me to merge with you?" I asked.

"Yes."

"And what would that mean?"

"It would be the wires of my being," she said, "and yours winding between us, inside of us. You would not only see my world but you would be of it. You would know what it would be like to be the monster you think I am."

"I don't think . . ."

Cylla Bene smiled at me and I didn't finish my lame defense.

"Why do you trust me if you know how I feel?" I asked.

"Because you fed me and sat next to me emitting sustenance for what you would call my soul." Cylla cocked her head to the side and gazed into my eyes. "Because even though I frighten you, you felt for me and created me."

I kissed her. I kissed her again and again crying and moaning. I put my arms around her and held on tight. Her voice held the tones of my mother and father and so many cousins and friends who might have held me when the world got too big.

"Are you going to change into something else, Cylla?" I asked then.

"No. Not for many eons. My world is a world of change. But this world has different laws. I can merge once, maybe twice, but I must return to this form for nourishment and rest. Ultimately this will be who and what I am."

"So you'll stay with me?"

"I'll go away now and then. But there's not much that will be expected of me. I was one of nine that were to make contact with the humans. But it is obvious that your rulers and thinkers do not want us. So we can, how do you say? Party."

"And while we're dancing the human race will fall into ruins?" I said.

"Only to rise again," Cylla added, "a phoenix from our loins."

She kissed me then. It was a lusty kiss, a triumphant kiss. She was my woman and I was the man scrambling after her: the apex of my desires.

Cylla yawned and laid back on the bed.

"Your feelings are subtle and strange, Raleigh Redman," she said. "My limbs need warmth and my eyes seek darkness."

"You're cold," I said pulling the blankets over her, "and tired. Close your eyes and the darkness will turn to sleep. And in a while, a few hours you will rise up warm and wide awake."

She smiled and made a kissing gesture and then she was off on her first night of sleeping.

While she slept I fretted.

I had never been unconditionally patriotic. Most people of color in the United States are cautious in their devotion to a nation that has always seen itself as a bastion of white European ascendancy. And black people descended from slaves know better than to expect a fair shake from our so-called democracy. From hiring practices to police harassment we have been given reasons every day to disassociate

ourselves from the heirs of American history—the secretly self-proclaimed masters.

That being said, America was the only country I'd ever known. Human beings had been, until that evening, the only intelligent life-form that I was aware of. Cylla wasn't threatening white America, she foretold the destruction of all nations and races. At this moment her fellows were organizing creatures to stand up against humanity and bring it down.

I believed that she could do what she prophesied. After all we had been warring against the Iraqi and Afghan peoples longer than we'd fought in World War II and we were definitely losing. And whatever beings the Ido would bring against us would not have national borders or human frailties. We would soon be bowing down to be beheaded by monsters.

I considered going to the authorities. The moment I had this thought Cylla turned over in her sleep. Her first dream, or maybe an intuition of my betrayal?

She bunched the foam pillow under her head and settled down.

And why shouldn't she settle back down to rest? I wasn't going to the authorities. They would have taken Cylla from me and studied her like a bug or a virus. And when I told them that her kind were organizing against humanity they would have arrested me, dropped hydrogen bombs on the ocean, declared war on countries we decided had been in collusion with the Alien Threat.

I wasn't patriotic but I might have been the last hope of the human race. I was smarter than our president because I knew I was powerless. I was wilier than many white men

and women because I knew that anybody, guilty or innocent, could wind up on death row . . . just because.

Cylla smiled in her sleep. She murmured something. I
touched her hair and kissed her cheek. She was my enemy
and I loved her. She was the most dangerous being on the
planet, maybe next to man, and yet she made me feel secure.

I touched her fingers and instinctively she took my hand.
This had a soporific effect on me. I lay down next to her
and dreamed of mountains with voices like an orchestra of
huge tubas rumbling through my body.

I WOKE UP LATE in the morning feeling whole and at
peace. The world was on the brink of disaster but that
didn't bother me much. Thousands upon millions of my
fellow humans were dying each day; terrible deaths from
disease and infected water, from famine or war. Peoples
hated each other and even the rich were winnowed down to
slender little lives that had no expanse or joy.

I turned to my side but Cylla wasn't there. An eon before, yesterday, I would have been clutched by fear that
she'd left me. But I wasn't afraid. Cylla was my woman. I
couldn't boss her around or beat her but she was mine.

"Hi, baby," she said from the doorway. "You slept late."

"How was your first night's sleep?" I asked her.

"Dreams," she said. "In a way the dreams of Man are
more free than the Merge of Life from my world. Loved ones
who live inside me lived again last night. They were awak-
ened and they counseled me."

"What did they say?" I asked.

She smiled, her Afro-golden face glowing with passion.

"That I should trust you and let you lead me if you can find the courage."

"I want to help" I said. "I want to be part of you."

Cylla held out her hand. I flinched and moved back from her.

"Not yet," I said. "I need a little while . . . just to get ready."

Cylla smiled and pulled her hand back.

"I love you, Raleigh Redman," she said.

I knew these words were true. There was no doubt in my mind that Cylla was my woman and that she would die for me. My life was not in danger. I would survive the holocaust that was coming, the destruction that humanity had thoughtlessly called upon itself.

"Yeah," I said. "I'm so lucky to have you here. I know it. I'm sorry about . . ."

"I understand," she said. "You need to be sure. All your life you've been looking for the moment when you could go beyond yourself. I feel your fear."

Again I was in the dream with the peasant woman and the insects gnawing their way toward us. I felt the fear again but this time I accepted it. I had been elevated by a moment of unconscious selflessness. I could have run from or attacked Cylla; I could have turned the beast in to the authorities— but I didn't do any of these things. Many people would have condemned me. But my mother's death and my father's alcoholism had detached me from society and so, contradictorily, I became their only hope.

"I'm going out for a while, Cylla," I said. "I want to walk and think. But let me give you my cell phone number. That way if you need me you can—"

Cylla placed her hand on mine and smiled.

"If I want you I just have to think about you," she said, "and if you want me all you have to do is say my name."

NICCI LIVED ON the Upper East Side of Manhattan at that time. It was a long way from my house but I decided to walk there. There was a lot on my mind but I wasn't the only one. There was fear and desolation, loneliness and grief on all sides as I walked up Third Avenue. There were women who hated men but wanted love and commitment from them and men who hated themselves but wanted approbation from any and all around them. There was pain both physical and psychological and a haze of melancholia that pervaded almost every man and woman, adolescent and child. I felt these currents of emotion as I walked. Humanity was far down on the evolutionary scale. Our aptitude to love and to see was no more than a furry mammalian reflex inherited from fishes, bacteria, and the pain of birth.

Cylla's world was so much beyond us that it was like a child's dream of God. Her world was magnificent, complete in itself for all that it was dying. For her people history was not thought but being. Time was not passing but traveling with everyone who lived and shared.

Cylla's world was dying but so was every human being I passed, or almost every one. Now and then a spirit would pass me smiling, hoping, happy with the sunshine and the weight of their bodies on their feet. Mostly babies and young mothers but some men too. There was hope for us. There was potential in our dismal, alienated hearts.

"WHO IS IT?" Nicci said in answer to my pressing her buzzer.

Her sixth-floor apartment was just west of First Avenue on Ninety-eighth Street.

"It's me," I said.

This declaration was met with an extended silence. Long seconds went by but I wasn't bothered by the migration of time. I had only glimpsed Cylla's world but I absorbed enough of her being to know that time was boundless even in a lower life-form like myself. Millions of years of evolution and experience resided within me. Even as I stood there I could feel the miles of blood vessels and nerves pulsing, retracing, replenishing. I could feel my personality changing, reverting, becoming.

"Rahl?" Nicci said over the tinny speaker.

"Yeah."

"Go down to Trio Coffee Shop on Second. I'll be there in a little while. Okay?"

"Okay."

I could hear the worry in her voice. And in that tone I heard so many things that I knew but never considered. Nicci had been drawn to me at a moment in between one step and the next in her life. She loved the fact that I needed her in order to be a man . . . or not even a man but at least something that approximated masculinity. The feelings I had for her I had never experienced before and she reveled in the passion that her touch aroused. I couldn't touch her, not like Tom Beam or Morley Tambor

or even Pete. The pleasure I brought to her was my weakness, my need.

I ORDERED A TRIPLE ESPRESSO with steamed cream on the side, a half-liter of sparkling water, and a plain scone with butter and strawberry jam. Trio had eight tables but only three of them were occupied. I sat there next to the window sipping my coffee feeling the errant emotions of people around me. A calmness had come over me that even the promise of lifelong wealth had not produced.

Cylla's love was something that grew from inside me and across a hitherto unknown universe. Just her being made me whole. And even though the world of Man was about to end I had never been happier.

I looked up and saw Nicci come in followed by Tom Beam.

Tom was tall and slender but strong. He was a white man, my age, who worked in finance doing something that made lots of money. His hair was dark and his eyes storming. I stood and held out a hand to him. He ignored the offer and sat down. When Nicci joined him I returned to my seat.

I looked at Nicci and she shrugged telling me with the gesture that she couldn't keep him away.

"Can I get you guys something?" the waitress asked. She'd come up while we three floated upon the dissonance of our own thoughts.

"No," Tom said.

"Latte," Nicci said, "with two shots."

When the waitress left Tom fixed me with an evil stare. He was a handsome man, probably a wonderful lover for

Nicci. He had a strong will and no intention of having my good luck steal his woman away.

He would have done better to stay at home, to wait until Nicci had helped me with my conundrum.

I gazed back into Tom's angry glare, my mind expanding to the size of redwoods, fairy-tale giants, and even mountains. I could feel Tom's consciousness fall into the vastness of Cylla's world. But I did not grab hold of him as she did with me. I did not love him or worry about his fears.

"What's going on, you guys?" Nicci asked.

But by that time Tom's hands were shaking. His neck shivered as if sub-zero fingers were caressing his neck. He made a sound like an animal trapped in the wild and then he stood up knocking the chair down behind him.

"Tom!" Nicci yelled.

But he didn't respond. He backed away and then ran out the door. Through the window at the side of the restaurant we could see him projectile vomiting into the street.

Nicci moved to rise but I caught her by the wrist.

"Leave him," I said.

"Let me go," Nicci shouted but then she looked into my eyes. Most of the Ido was gone from my gaze but the little that was left arrested her. She sat, staring at me while Tom Beam fell to the sidewalk, into his own vomit, and then got up and started running.

"What's happened to you, Rahl?"

I let go her wrist looking away.

"What do you want, Nicci?" I asked.

"What do you mean? From you?"

"From life," I said. "Do you ever look up in the clouds and want to be up there, floating?"

An angry scowl crossed Nicci's face. Her lips twisted as if she'd just bitten into something rotten.

"Are you crazy?" she asked.

"I thought you'd broken up with Tom."

"I was lonely. You just told me that I was a whore."

"No," I said. "I said that I was brokenhearted. I was your dog, Nicci, but I couldn't see it. I've been seeing things lately."

"Like the sky?"

"Yeah." I couldn't help but grin.

"I don't get it," Nicci said. "What did you do to Tom?"

"I don't know."

"Why did you come to my apartment? To see if I was in there with some other guy?"

"No. I don't care about that," I said. "I met a girl. I love her. I just wanted to ask you a question."

"What girl? What question? The one about the clouds?"

"Kinda? Do you . . ." I stopped a moment realizing that I didn't have the words to explain or betray Cylla.

"I have to make a decision," I said.

"What kind of decision?"

"My girlfriend—"

"What's this girl's name?" Nicci asked.

"Cylla. Cylla Bene."

"Italian?"

"She's not from America, no."

"Does she have a green card?"

"I don't think so."

"And so she wants you to marry her so she can stay here," Nicci concluded.

"Something like that."

"She's after your money, Rahl."

"Money doesn't mean a thing to Cylla," I said.

"How do you know?"

"Everybody has been after my money, Nick," I said using the pet name I hadn't uttered in two years. "I know it when it's coming at me. Pete was after my money and, and you were too."

"Me?"

"Come on, Nicci," I said. "You only called me after I won the lottery. You called every day. You never did that even when we were together."

"Take it back," she said.

I saw the implacable anger in her. Nicci didn't want me to say the truth out loud. She had the power to make me into a man and I had the money to make her life easier, but neither one of us wanted to have these truths said aloud.

"Okay," I said. "Yeah. But let me ask you something."

"What?"

"Let's say that Cylla isn't after my money. Let's say that she only wants to come here because she needs to."

"Why would she need to?"

"Because people are dying where she's from. Because if she comes here she might be able to bring her family."

Nicci's eyebrows knitted and her mouth made that little pout that I once loved.

"This is serious, isn't it?" she asked.

"Yeah."

"Is this a black girl?"

"I guess so. Yeah. What they call a person of color."

"I thought you liked white girls, Rahl."

"You know my problem, Nicci. You know that color don't mean a thing if you can't get the feeling."

"And this Cylla does that for you?"

"She makes my toes curl and my soul quiver," I said in a tone that pushed Nicci back in her chair.

We sat there staring at each other. I was happy that for the first time since I'd known Nicci I wasn't her subordinate, her junior partner, her grateful, submissive sex slave.

"Why come to me, Rahl?" she asked. "Is there something wrong with this chick?"

After a moment of contemplation I nodded.

"There's something wrong with her?" Nicci asked.

"I don't know why I came to you," I said. "I mean, I mean I do know but it's not right. I mean you're the only person I ever knew who made me feel like I was there. You know what I mean?"

"No, baby," Nicci said. "Not at all."

That was what I was waiting to hear. Maybe Nicci never loved me the way I did her but she had been there in my life. She had seen me for what I was. But even she could not touch me or know me.

"Can I do anything for you, Nick?" I said.

"Like what?"

"Anything."

"You could pay my tuition for the next four years."

"Done."

WE PARTED AT THE CORNER of Ninety-eighth and Second Avenue. I watched her walk away with my check for

sixty thousand dollars in her jeans pocket. When I turned around Cylla was standing there.

"I'm ready," I said.

"I know."

WE WALKED BACK to my little apartment holding hands like teenagers. Now and then Cylla would kiss my cheek or my knuckle and smile for me as I had always wanted someone to smile.

"You could be seducing me," I said at Forty-second Street and Lexington Avenue.

"No."

"Why not?"

"You'll see," she said and she put her arm around my waist.

I'm not a powerful man. Neither am I handsome or charismatic. The reason I had loved Nicci was because she made feel those things. But Cylla was different; she was a god who needed an acolyte in order to be. We were inseparable, the inside of the stone and the outside too.

WE SAT NEXT TO EACH OTHER on my vinyl blue sofa. Her eyes were bright with expectation.

"Are you ready?" she asked.

"I guess."

"We can wait."

"But if we do all those people we passed on the street may die."

Cylla was growing into her beauty, transforming as I got to know her better. She was becoming what I needed as these needs changed. She was like a human god, one whose face alters with the times.

"When we fuck," she said, "you come into me. You fill me with your manhood. Now, when I touch you," she said, pressing her palm against my chest, "I will enter you. I will make you part of what I am."

I had never been more afraid. Tremors moved through me uncontrollably. I was about to ask her to wait a few moments when something like a blunted spear pierced my chest. I cried out but the sound was drowned in a paroxysm of pain. I closed my eyes and felt myself dying. My heart stopped as did my breath. I could feel Cylla climbing into me, donning me like a suit of clothes. Her hands filled mine. Her head pressed up against my brain. And all the while I was screaming from my soul.

But even in this distress I was aware of the feeling of my soul, the soul. It was an experience outside of the corporeal. I was something beyond matter and beyond myself. There was no separation, no disunity.

I was definitely dying, fading away as I lay down on my back upon the sofa. As my life ended I remembered that I wanted to buy a new sofa now that I was rich.

My eyes were wide and Cylla was gone from the room. My bowels released and time stopped completely. The world, everything had drained to gray.

"Come," she whispered.

"You killed me," I replied though I had no breath to utter these words.

"Yes. Now come."

"I'm dead."

"Life is nothing but a dance at the end of the hangman's rope," she said. "There is something more."

A turquoise patina infused the gray world at the edges of my vision.

"You killed me," I said with no emotion, vibration, or intention.

"That's like a table complaining about being dusted," she said, "a sheet worrying about being hung out to dry."

"Life is all we have," I argued without conviction.

"It is only a step between one place and another."

And then I was released from my body. I was everywhere and anything. I was soaring but not like a bird or breeze. There was a roaring sound all around.

"What is that?" I asked Cylla.

"It is the roar of the world," she said. "It is a step beyond."

"You murdered me," I said.

"No. I merely killed your body so that you could see what is happening to your world."

The ontological (this is a word that I picked up from my studies, it means "the basis for reality") experience of soul-drifting is hard to get at in human terms much less human words. When we experience the world as finite beings lashed to physical bodies we have a focal point, a place in the scheme of things. But when Cylla took me from my body I was nowhere, everywhere, connected to long tiers of being that took the place of planets and solar systems, atoms and quarks.

It was as if the totality of the universe was an enormous Word that took forever to pronounce. This Word thundered

through my mind revealing past and present, here and there. And I was not only the Listener but also a sound at the beginning of a minor syllable. I was part of a greater being that was, and was not, of the world I knew.

But I was also wedded to Cylla. I knew her and her peoples all the way back to the beginning of my people's time. She was my heart and she had enunciated the Word and so knew it in all of its possibilities and failings.

The Word said things that were sometimes true and sometimes not true because they were possibilities that conflicted with the odds. My mind was too small to know everything that my other self, Cylla, knew. Forms took shape in my sphere of comprehension and I was among them jostled about like an infant being moved from hand to hand.

THE CLEET WERE A BREED of yellow and green and red birds, parrots that lived in a small area along the Amazon. Their minds were avian and sharp, in many ways superior to human intelligence. They were large birds, half a pound or more each with sharp claws and a fierce love for their kind.

The Ido bundle that had appeared among the Cleet was immediately accepted as a gift from beyond. The Cleet's ability to see was akin to the soul-drifting that Cylla had shown me. They merged with their visitor after only two days of deliberation and now they were multiplying, altering, getting ready for war . . .

———

IN THE OCEAN an Ido bundle floated next to an eleven-foot bottle-nosed dolphin. They became lovers as Cylla and I had and now they were singing, calling for the migration of ten thousand more from Cylla's world . . .

IN MALI, ON A DESOLATE RISE, a bundle appeared to a colony of what would come to be known as Necrom Ants. The mindless creatures swarmed over the eighty-pound pole-snake, stroking it like a new queen. But instead of eggs that alien merged with millions of the tiny beings, their souls sparkling in the African night like a sky filled with stars . . .

"THEY ARE ALL calling to my people," Cylla-I said.

"To invade Earth?" I asked.

"To save Ido."

"Kill humanity?"

"Not if we become Man."

While we conversed in single sentences the universe spoke its name among all possibilities both realized and failed. Colors and memories, impossible meetings and simple void rocked me, me: flotsam—both pedestrian and divine.

The next thing I knew I was taking in a ragged breath. Cylla was standing over me. There was a hole in my T-shirt and blood everywhere—on the couch and my clothes, down my arms and on the floor.

Cylla's golden eyes fixed me there.

"You killed me," I said, feeling definite sexual gratification.

"I resurrected you," she said.

"I heard the word 'war,' " I said.

"Will you try to convince your people to join us?"

I sat up and opened my hands, the tacky feel of drying blood between my fingers, covering me—my blood. I remembered the possible futures of the Earth: swarms of Cleet, from the size of small hens to huge land-bound racing monsters, slaughtering soldiers and children alike; armored dolphins sinking one ship after another from South Africa to the North Pole; and ants using their sublime architecture to bring down the edifices of man.

I picked up my yellow phone, marking it with dark red blood, and entered a number I'd known since the age of eight.

"Hello?"

"How much do you need, Pete?"

"Rahl?"

"Yeah."

"You gonna shoot me, man?" my childhood friend asked.

"No. I broke up with Nicci again. She told me about you to hurt me. I don't care 'bout that shit though."

Pete was always wondering how he would die. When we were children he'd regale us with long stories about how he'd die on a battlefield after saving American troops from certain defeat at the hands of the Chinese. For some irrational reason he hated the Chinese.

He was worried about dying but that didn't stop him from having sex with my girlfriend. He was pretty much perpetually unemployed. He probably came over while I was at work.

"Don't tell Rahl, okay, Pete?" I could hear Nicci say.

"Rahl?" Pete said on the phone.

"Yeah?"

"You not gonna shoot me are you, man?"

"How about twenty thousand dollars?" I said.

"No lie?"

"Straight up."

While I spoke Cylla raised her arms and one of her siblings appeared in the room, standing and quivering as Cylla had done only a few days before.

"What you want me to do?" Pete said in my ear.

"I want you to meet somebody." I handed the phone to Cylla.

While she spoke I went to the kitchen corner to get an apple for my guest.

"Hello?" Cylla said and then she listened. "Hi, Pete. My name's Cylla. I'm Raleigh's girlfriend. We want you to come over here so we can talk to you . . ."

AFTER CYLLA GOT OFF THE PHONE we started cleaning up my couch and the floor around it. Cylla was really an expert at cleaning. While I showered and then disposed of my soiled clothes she flooded the floor again and again until the blood was little more than a mild stain.

AN HOUR LATER there was a knock at my door. Cylla went to answer it.

"Hi," she said as human as could be, "you must be Pete."

Pete was both tall and fat. He wore a red exercise suit with yellow lines down the seams of his pants. He was worried

that my invitation might be a trap and so the moment he was
in the door I handed him an envelope filled with cash that I
hoarded in my mattress.

He ripped the wrapper and counted the cash, all in fifties, twice.

"This a lotta fuckin' money," he said while counting. He
said it more than once.

When he'd finished counting he shoved the money in his
red satin pocket. It looked like he had an apple in there.

"Why you burnin' incense?" he asked.

"All that sex Rahl make me do," Cylla said like a girl from
the hood. "He was embarrassed that you might smell it."

Pete grinned and then asked, "What you want from me,
man?"

"Let's sit down, Pete," Cylla said.

My oldest friend looked at the young woman with hunger in his eyes. Her beauty was growing still. But I wasn't
worried about losing her, no more than I feared losing my
hands or elbows.

Cylla and Pete sat on the blue sofa while I pulled up a
straight-back chair. Pete's unspoken emotions were all
across his face. He was afraid for his safety after having
admitted sleeping with my last girlfriend. On the other
hand he had more money in his pocket than he'd ever had
at one time before. He wanted to spend that money, not sit
in some stuffy little apartment.

He was also acutely aware of Cylla. She wore blue jeans
and a red halter top that she'd bought while I was talking
to Nicci and Tom. Her figure, her skin, her eyes made a
man want to get closer, and closer.

"You got yourself one fine girlfriend here, Rahl," he said with a savoring smile.

"You hear about them things they call 'pole-snakes'?" I asked while he clutched his pocket and gawped.

"Uh-huh."

"What if I told you that she was one of them?"

Cylla shifted on the sofa moving her bustline in a satisfying arc.

"I'd say the snake done shucked its skin an' lemme at her."

Pete actually licked his lips.

"I'm not lyin', brother," I said in a tone of voice that turned Pete's head.

Staring at me he said, "You mean this was one'a them sticks blew up Moscow and them chinks in Mongol Land?"

I nodded.

"You tryin' to tell me she not a real girl?" Pete pressed his back against the sofa.

Cylla stood up and turned around, slowly. My friend's eyes got bigger.

"She was what I'd always dreamed of and because I fed her and cared for her she became my dream."

"What you feed her?" Pete asked.

Cylla sat down before him like a golden, hip-hop diva.

"Apples and pears," I said.

"What you want from me?"

"I have a sister," Cylla said, "who needs you to feed her and make her dreams real. She needs you to make her into your ideal, whatever that is."

"Will it hurt?" he asked.

"I did it," I said in answer. I had always been the weakest of us three; afraid of pain and danger. The only thing Pete was afraid of was the moment of his death; Frank, for all I knew, feared nothing.

"And I could keep this money?" Pete asked.

"I'll add another twenty thousand in a few weeks," I said, knowing that in a few weeks the world of humanity would have already begun its transformation.

A period of silence ensued. Pete wanted my woman, my money, and some dream that he'd had forever. He was hungry for a life outside his mother's apartment and the countless bosses that always let him go.

He'd been my friend since I was a stuttering child in the third grade. We laughed together every day and shared our dreams of power and sex. As we got older those hopes faded into street talk and kung fu bravado. Only Frank talked about the larger world after a while. And even he never did all that much. He'd sit back in his recliner and complain but he didn't actually *do* anything, never tried to become more than what he was.

"What I gotta do?" Pete asked. His fat cheeks quivered and his eyes were no longer on Cylla's figure.

"Bring it out, baby," I said to Cylla.

My lover, Miss Bene leaped up from the blue vinyl and skipped into the bedroom.

"Where you get a girlfriend that fine, man?" Pete asked as soon as she had disappeared. "She like the finest thing I ever seen."

"Yeah. I guess I wanted somebody that everybody else want too," I said aware that the language I was using was of the streets where we spent our childhoods.

Cylla returned with the Ido bundle in her arms. She didn't seem to be straining under the weight like I had. I wondered how strong Cylla was. She smiled at me and dumped the saplinglike flaccid beast on the sofa next to Pete.

He inched away while Cylla came to rest on my lap.

"What, what you want me to do wit' it?" he asked.

"Lay a hand on it," Cylla said.

"What hand?"

"It doesn't matter."

"It bite?"

"No."

Pete turned to me then, the fear active in his gaze.

"What's gonna happen if I do this?" he asked.

"It won't hurt you," I assured him.

"No?"

"You will see things that you never imagined," I said. "What you wished for in your secret mind will come to you and grow with you."

"And what if I say no?"

"You know too much to say no," Cylla replied, her voice hard as some infinitely reflective, unbreakable jewel.

It occurred to me that she promised not to merge without acceptance but that she said nothing about refraining from murder.

"What you mean by that, girl?" Pete said.

"Just lay your hand on the Ido," Cylla purred. "It will not bite you."

Pete turned to me but all I did was hunch my shoulders. I had not intended for Pete to get in the sights of murder but there we were and so the game had to be played out.

"This is it, Pete," I said. "This where they separate the men from the niggahs. This where the fat hits the fire."

"You do it?"

"Yes I did."

"Did it hurt?"

"I'm here, ain't I," I said, avoiding the answer as well as I could.

I was angry at my friend. He had betrayed me the way humans do. But I was no longer completely human. I saw the world the way humans do. I breathed and bled, spoke and loved but I also saw nebulae in my fingertips and billions of dead women, children, and men at my feet. I may have hated Pete but he was one of the keys to salvation. There was no room for petty payback.

Pete raised his hand and moved it gingerly toward the barklike flesh of the wheezing Ido.

"What's that sound?" Pete asked.

"Breath," Cylla hissed.

Again Pete moved his fingers toward the slumped bundle. When he touched the lower half a spark was struck. Quickly Pete pulled his fat hand away.

"It tickles!"

"You're teasing her," Cylla said. "She wants your caress."

Pete was breathing hard. Sweat shone on his onyx-colored face. His eyes were bulging, there was a whimper coming from deep in his chest. I was sure that he was going to jump up and run from the room. As I have said, my friend was plagued by the fear of death and dreams of heroism; a man afraid of the darkness in his own shadow but who also wanted to die in glorious battle.

He slapped his hand down on the Ido bundle, pole-snake, interdimensional visitor, explorer, invader.

Pete's body went rigid and his eyes honed down to slits. He began mumbling to himself.

"What's this? Wha-? Hey, man. Hey look at that, that . . . what is it? Oh my God. Oh my God."

"Did I sound like that?" I asked Cylla.

"You were silent, my love."

"He seems so scared," I said.

This was an understatement. Pete was quivering, jittering, now moaning out loud. From its "mouth" the Ido bundle's long white tubes emerged. Slowly they moved toward my friend who was at once ecstatic and catatonic. The first tube shot out, piercing Pete's forehead. The second white worm penetrated his chest near where his heart was. As the third "tooth" cut into his thigh, the first emerged from the back of his skull, looped around, and bored into the top of his spine. Blood was flowing from each wound. Pete stiffened, took a quick breath, and died right there before me.

I was dimly aware that Cylla had risen and headed toward the bathroom. I couldn't turn away from the sight before me:

When I'd fed Cylla she used those tubes to suck the nutrients and pulp of the fruits. This time the opposite was happening. This time, as the long white tubes pumped, the bundle was getting smaller, transferring its mass into Pete. His already huge body was inflating, getting larger and larger.

Cylla came in with a mop and bucket and started cleaning the blood from the floor around them.

"What are you doing?" I asked.

"Cleaning up after them," she said simply.

"But look at it."

"It's just blood," the lover of my entire life said. "Blood and other fluids that make men and Ido, fish and fowl."

Her eyes glittered. In my peripheral vision I could see that the bundle had shrunk down to the size and shape of a football. Pete was bloated like one of the corpses in Rwanda left out in the hot sun too long. His eyes were wide and blank. His mouth was open and his tongue protruded.

Cylla went to empty her bucket.

The white "teeth" of the Ido bundle lurched and emptied the rest of the alien being into my dead friend; they followed entering his body like flopping spaghetti being sucked down by a hungry diner. Now all that was left was my oldest friend bloated half again his size.

I'd seen dead people in my life; my father in his casket, a guy on Forty-fourth Street who was stabbed just a few minutes before I passed by, and Mrs. Simon my seventh-grade teacher who had a heart attack in the hall while I was passing from one class to another.

Mrs. Simon was a white lady but she turned blue when she died. I was so upset that night that my father gave me a shot of whiskey so that I'd forget and go to sleep. But I dreamed about Mrs. Simon. She was getting up from the concrete floor in front of Sarah Knorr's locker. She was smiling and borrowed my handkerchief to wipe the blue from her face.

I'd seen death enough to know that Pete was dead.

I began to wonder about my own death only a few hours before. What was I now if I had died like Pete? Maybe I

wasn't me. Maybe Cylla had disposed of Raleigh Redman and now I was just a memory doing her bidding. Maybe I was dead, had died and been resurrected like in the Bible's fortelling of the future.

"No," she whispered in my ear. "You are alive and well and safe from everything you ever feared."

Her words calmed me. I wanted to think more about what dying like Pete would mean to my soul but I could not keep my mind on that line of thought. Cylla was as close to me as my heart and mind; she was an ally that would never turn. I trusted her even though I didn't want to.

While having these thoughts Pete's chest split open, emitting a loud cracking noise; it was the sound of bones breaking. From his insides an amber-skinned Asian woman rose. She was small of stature but lovely and wild-eyed. Her skin was shiny with the gore of Pete's insides. When she saw us she grinned like a madwoman just released from some medieval asylum.

"I am Gorda," she said, holding her hands out to me.

I took her hands and held them even though they were slick with my friend's blood.

"Hi," I said, trying to keep from vomiting.

"Don't worry, Rahl," Gorda said. "Pete knows what you have done for him. He does not regret."

Cylla came up to her sister then.

"Let's wash you up," she said to Gorda.

She took the newly reborn by the hand and led her into the bathroom. When they were gone I felt as if it all might have been a dream except for the blasted corpse of my oldest friend on the sofa, and the bloody footprints that led from him into the toilet.

I fell into my straight-back chair and sat vigil over Pete. I could still see the bulge of the money in his red satin pocket. I was numb. I was looking at Pete but not seeing him, at least not clearly. I was trying to go back over the past few days, trying to understand how it could have been different.

The water in the shower had come on. I had the instant flash of a million ants attacking an army vehicle. Black men, soldiers were screaming and running from the tank. There were a dozen or more dying under the cover of biting, stinging insects.

Beyond the screams of those men I heard a loud snapping noise.

Pete's bones were pulling inward, his tongue sucked back into his mouth. In the next thirty seconds his body repaired itself completely. First bone, then sinew, then his skin knitted together. Pete gasped and sat straight up on the couch. His eyes were wide and he'd lost at least a hundred pounds.

"I died," he said.

I nodded.

"Gorda killed me."

"You know her name?" I asked.

"Know it? Damn I been thinkin' 'bout that girl since the sixth grade. She was the girl I wanted for me."

"But she's Asian," I said.

"Chinese," Pete said, correcting me. "I know it's crazy but I cain't help that."

The bathroom door opened and Gorda came out, still naked but now clean. She and Pete embraced and kissed. He fell to his knees with his arms around her waist and she put her hands on his head smiling as if this was all she would ever need.

"They are one," Cylla said, putting her arm around my shoulders.

"Men are dying in Africa," I told my lover.

"Men have been slaughtering themselves since the beginning," she said. "And before that other creatures fought and destroyed from instinct or for survival."

"Will it be over?" I asked.

"One way or another," Cylla replied.

Pete and Gorda stumbled into my bathroom, embracing and laughing as they went. The shower came on again and I imagined her washing the blood from her lover. Ten minutes later they lurched naked from the toilet into my bedroom. I didn't resent their presumption. I could see how much they needed to be together. I had had the same experience with Cylla.

While they made love Cylla and I washed off the sofa and floor and then sat there, holding hands.

My mind was like some impossible sculpture made from steel and fire, water and the vacuum of space. I loved Cylla. Looking into her eyes I saw myself encased in a transparent, glistening globe of knowledge: her awareness of me. She was there only for me. If I had asked her to forget the rest of the world and the Ido transition she would have done so without a second thought. But I was still a man in a world of women and men who were doomed if I did not act. I wanted to do something but those golden eyes arrested me.

In the background I could hear Pete and Gorda making love. It didn't bother me. It didn't excite me. Together Cylla and I had brought life into the world.

"Why did she come to me first?" I asked.

"You mean why did Gorda hold her hands out to you?"

"Yes."

"You are the Prime One in the human cycle of the transition," she said. "We must all answer to you."

"I'm like a leader?"

"You are the first among equals. You brought life here for your people and so you are the instrument of humanity's hope."

"So is there a Cleet bird like me and a Prime Ant in Mali?"

"The Cleet have a Prime Commune as the ants have a Prime Hive led by their ultimate queen. You are more like Dolphus the seagoing mammal who even now is collecting his people far beneath the waves of your ocean."

"Don't you miss your world, Cylla? I mean here you are just a human with arms and legs and eyes. What were you on your world?"

Cylla smiled at me then.

"I was what you would call a Touchstone, where the Crystal River flowed into the Cerulean Sea. Those travelers who passed would reach out to impart their experiences into me. I would in turn release knowledge that they needed for their journeys."

"How long?"

"Time is a difficult subject for us to express. Before I was the Touchstone I was a part of Mountains of Power and before that I was a grain of sand in the Desert of Reflection. My memories go all the way back to the beginning of time where there was one thought—hunger."

"How long ago was that?" I asked wanting to know everything about my alien lover. All her knowledge was already in

me but when she spoke I could see what she said and know what she meant in human terms.

"There was no life on your world when I first became aware," she said.

"But that means that you are a god, Cylla. I am nothing next to you." I released her hands and she reached out for me again.

"You are the Prime One and we are mere wastrels looking for homes across the billion billion planes. Gorda and I and ten thousand others will come to you and you will be our Touchstone, our open arms."

"How?"

"I am yours," she said.

"Like a slave?"

"No. Like a child or an arm or an idea you use to understand the seasons."

"And what do I do with you?" I asked.

"Bring my ten thousand siblings to your world. Make them familiar with your people and we will be the vanguard for the larger transition."

I was about to ask what that transition might be but the thought appeared in my mind. At at least three points throughout the world alien cities were going to appear. In the Sahara Desert, the Pacific Ocean, and Brazil huge buildinglike structures would be constructed. Inside each of these a million Ido bundles would lie dormant for a decade; while man and other life-forms organized themselves for the possibility of merging species.

Three cities and maybe a fourth if I could raise an army of human Ido.

"And I am the first spokesman for the human race?" I asked.

"Yes."

"Why? I'm nobody. I'm nothing in the vast history of the world."

"You saved me. You made me into a dream of mankind. Like a seed blowing on the wind you fell to fertile ground and will propagate your species. It was luck. It was fate. It doesn't matter because here we are."

Pete groaned from the other room and Gorda said something; I couldn't make out the words but they sounded Chinese.

"Shall we make love?" Cylla asked, her hand stoking my neck lightly.

I thought that there were important jobs for us to do, that we had to get to work, but Cylla's gentle touch and innocent offer were like twin butterflies dancing on the first day of summer. I leaned over to kiss her and fell, happily.

While the Cleet planned their aerie, while the ants destined to be known as Necrom Ants burrowed deep under the Saharan desert creating tunnels a meter in diameter and hundreds of miles long, while Dolphus sang his song of merging in high sweet tones heard throughout the Pacific Ocean—Cylla and I made love on the blue vinyl sofa. She was astride me looking into my eyes, becoming more and more human as I drifted away from the humanity I had learned about in public schools and on city streets, from lying newspapers and the arrogance of our warlike genes.

"I could do this forever," she whispered when I was spent and could do no more.

"Merge with me," I said.

"But it hurts you," Cylla said. "We are already wedded. You do not have to suffer again."

"Merge with me, Cylla. And this time go deep, go all the way so that I can be you for just a while."

"But why?"

"For my people."

The first time Cylla entered through my chest like the shunt of a blunted spear thrown by a giant. But this time it was as if she were salt and I was the delicate flesh of a snail melting, disintegrating under the acid created by our contact. I wasn't dead. I didn't exist, had never existed. I could see Cylla's life like an open flower releasing its scent into a world of blossoms and trees, spores and pollens. There was unity in my dissolution. The world was one great cooperative passing its knowledge easily and flawlessly from one being to another. There was no vestige of earthly life with its continual conflicts and crimes, politics based on selfish ends, laws made to enslave. Our world, Earth; was a place of conflict and death. These concepts, though extant in the history of Ido, were far in the past. In very recent time the Ido had experienced conflict once again because of the cancer that grew, the gray withering that started in the southern part of their world.

I imagined a glistening black globe the size of a one-family house, resembling the body of a black widow spider, falling to land. Whether the malignance was solely in that meteorite or somehow the life of Ido mutated and turned in on itself after being exposed is not known but the planet is slowly being eroded. It's unity of life dissolving.

The totality of this experience was so complete that I wanted to stay there with Cylla, with all the varied and

interconnected minds of her world. Life on Earth for me meant nothing. I reached out with my soul to her world.

"No."

I wanted nothing more than to be a blade of grass at base of her, the Touchstone. I could be a fluttery crystal wing floating through the sky destined to become a mountain or the germ of a single thought.

"No."

I could fight the gray withering death. I knew what it was to struggle and battle. All the Ido knew was how to come together.

"No."

With all my heart and being I strained to stay in the dream of the Ido. The Ido where *I* was also *we,* where past was now and future held no shadows. Ido, where mind was not certainty but musical improvisation that never stopped playing to a world where dance and breath were one.

WHEN I OPENED MY EYES I was on the floor. Pete and Cylla and Gorda sat around me. They all had their hands on me. They seemed worried.

"What's wrong?" I asked.

"We almost lost you, brothah," Pete said.

This made me smile. He was looking down on me, caring maybe for the first time about who I was and what I felt.

"We were never friends before were we, Pete?"

"How could we be, man? We didn't know nuthin'."

Gorda moved her hand up higher on my thigh. It was then that I realized I was naked.

"You drifted after a place that is only in our minds," Pete's ideal woman said to me. "You would have disappeared if we had not held on to you."

I felt their psychic embrace still. It was as if I were being tethered by webbing or thick glue. Inwardly I sighed, realizing that the dream of Ido would never be a reality for me. I was of the belligerent Earth, child of violence and dysfunction. My only hope was to transform my world as Ido life had informed me.

I stood up feeling strong and hopeful. Cylla had brought me clean clothes. I dressed quickly while my friends talked in low tones. The world was in my hands and with every motion I felt history being made.

"Ready to go?" I said to Pete.

"Let's hop to it," Pete replied.

THE GIRLS SAID that they would take a walk while we attended to business.

On the street my old-new friend and I walked slowly, side by side. He was slimmer, darker skinned by a shade or two. He'd put on one of my suits because his clothes were destroyed by the transition. There was a smile on his face. Pete kept looking around at strangers and dogs on leashes, at birds fluttering and even at zipping insects here and there.

"Do you think that we've been brainwashed?" I asked him.

"Brainwashed?" he declared. "Here you done died twice in one day and you worried about bein' brainwashed?"

"Do you think they're tryin' to use us to take over the world?" I said.

"No. Do you?"

"I have to ask, man. What we're doin' is serious shit here. Once it gets started it's not gonna stop."

"It's already started, brothah. It's already that."

HILDA ARDMAN ANSWERED our knock. She was light brown in color but her facial features were thick and clearly delineated like so many Africans who came here as baggage. She was lovely and bound to Frank Vell just as surely as if she were his slave.

"Yes?" she said in the tone one would use on door-to-door zealots or bill collectors. There was no recognition of the dozens of times we had knocked on that fourth-floor door and come in to watch a football game or boxing match.

"We here to see Frank," Pete said.

Somewhere a whale was pressing itself from the ocean and coming down with deadly force on a fishing vessel owned by a company that's main office was not two miles from where we stood. The boat was shattered and most of the crew killed. The whale, known to us as Oceanus, swam away looking for more serial killers that stalked in his world.

"Did he call you?" Hilda asked.

"This is very important, Hildy," I said. "Frank needs to see us right now."

"I don't know who the hell you think you are, Raleigh Redman, walkin' into my house tellin' me what my man need to do . . ."

Frank came up behind Hilda. I like to think that he sensed our mission at his door. I could hear the sports announcer

in the background yelling about some pass or dunk or left hook. People were cheering on the big speakers Frank had attached to his sixty-inch flat-panel plasma TV.

"It's okay, baby," the tall, ugly man said.

"I told 'em they just couldn't come drop in on us like they owned the place," Hilda said.

Frank put a hand on her shoulder and she went silent.

Hilda hadn't looked closely at Pete and me. She hadn't seen our physical, much less our internal changes. Hilda, as the old saying goes, only had eyes for her man.

But Frank saw the changes immediately.

"You lost that weight," he said to Pete. "And you been workin' out, Rahl."

We didn't say anything at first. Pete was looking into Frank's eyes. I was thinking about a dolphin incarnating a whale while a hundred thousand parrots beat their way across the rain forest darkening the sky with their ever-increasing numbers.

Frank was staring intently at us as Hilda shifted under his touch.

I had always understood that Frank had been our spiritual guide; I saw now that he still was. I could see in him the leader wanting to come out. But that chief had somehow been stymied by teachers who were also traitors, parents who were fools, and friends who could never understand his vision. And so he sat in front of the TV watching games but seeing the great movement of humanity across the field of human failure.

"We need to talk, brothah," Pete said.

"Alone," I added.

"Fuck you, Rahl," Hilda said.

"Baby, I got some important business with these men here," Frank said gently. "It ain't their fault. I need a few minutes alone."

"I could pack my bags and leave you alone for good."

All Frank had to do was catch her eye with his and she reached out for him, regretting her words only seconds after uttering them.

"Go on now," he said and she went shouldering her way between me and Pete out the front door.

Frank stood aside and we walked in. We made our way to the living room where Frank's lounging chair was set in front of a soccer game. I picked up his complex remote control and switched to a station that was covering the pole-snake debacle twenty-four hours a day. Human beings might not know everything but they knew enough to be afraid of us.

Us.

Two more pole-snakes had been discovered. One was caught in the act of attacking an old woman in Lima, Peru. The neighbors heard her screams and hacked the attacker to bits before it could burrow into her body. The woman died. Another of my siblings had appeared to a priest in Vatican City. Catholicism's version of the secret service had ended that possibility with holy fire.

"You a news junkie now that you a millionaire?" Frank asked me.

I realized that Pete and I had been so captivated by the stories that we were ignoring the man we came to see.

"We love you, Frank," I said. "You always knew what to do and what not to. You helped everybody even though you never gave a damn about us."

Frank was wearing a tan leisure suit that he'd owned for at least five years. He reached into the breast pocket and came out with a pair of thick-lensed glasses. As long as I'd known him I'd never seen Frank wearing glasses; the vanity of ugly men.

"Love? What's goin' on, Raleigh?" he asked.

"Those pole-snakes are like people, Frank. They're smart and they're here. People been killin' 'em but I didn't. I fused together with one and now I can see right through the sun."

I didn't know Frank. I didn't know anybody. My whole life had been spent looking for sugar and money and a place to lay my head. I was the dregs at the bottom of a coffee cup trying to imagine what it was like to be cream.

"You too, Pete?" Frank asked our once-fat friend.

A troop of soldiers in Sudan were walking past a new hive of Necrom Ants. The insects were absolutely still, waiting for the answer to a dream.

"Yeah, Frank. Raleigh pulled me in."

"What you see?" Frank asked.

"All the way back to when there was only one way, one thing. You an' me was there, Frank, all the way back then."

A sense of Ido elation went through me as I realized how much more there was for me to learn. I thought like Pete and knew many of the same things but, as an Ido, we were each part of a greater whole.

"And what are you?" Frank asked me.

"The leader," I said with no pride or arrogance.

"And you want me to follow you?"

"I want you to do what you do, Frankie. And I don't plan to stand in your way."

Frank was the smartest of us. He was frozen in place but

wise like a dead language that no one understood, least of all him.

"What if I say no?"

Pete looked at the door and I shook my head. Frank smiled at the threat of death.

"I'm your friend so you gonna kill me?" he asked.

"It's time to get off your ass, Frank," I said. "Time to turn off the damn TV and get busy."

The threat of death did not shake Frank as much as these words did. He bit his lower lip hard and then he nodded, slipped on his loafers, and stood up.

"Okay, my niggahs," he said, "let's go."

GORDA AND CYLLA HAD RETURNED and collected another Ido bundle by the time we'd gotten home. Frank didn't need to be bribed, seduced, or threatened. He walked up to the wavering branch and embraced it like it was a floating log on a stormy sea. They blended almost immediately and fell to the floor with a loud thump. There they writhed like their media namesakes. Soon they were a great brown mass. Every now and then Frank's head would rise from the ooze, a swimmer gulping down air in a race for his life.

The gyration of both Ido and human became more and more intense until it looked as if there were a battle raging on my floor. Gorda and Cylla clasped hands and Pete got down on his knees watching the struggle closely.

I wasn't worried. Frank's mind contained a strategist's intellect; the Ido would have to struggle to merge with that. But it was what they needed. He would make the plan that would save us.

Us. My mind had broadened to think of an us beyond black people, men, or humankind in general. My us was now Cleet and Necrom, Oceanus and a world so far away that there weren't enough subatomic particles in the abacus of my body to count the light-years.

After two long hours the struggle finally came to an end. The bundle and Frank burst apart leaving Frank on one side of the floor with a great gray wolf opposite him. The wolf was up immediately. First it ran to me and pressed my thigh with its snout, then it went to Frank licking his face and whining for him to awaken. The wolf's left eye was platinum and her right one gold.

Frank sat up quickly. He looked the same only now he was fuller in his body and handsome like the devil would be if he deigned to take on human form.

"The Prime One, huh?" he said with a smirk on his lips. "You always were a lucky motherfucker, Rahl."

THAT NIGHT FRANK DETAILED his strategy to conquer and save the human race.

"We got to get out of New York fast," Frank said. The two hours he spent struggling with Yaw, his wolf-sister, he'd been thinking about how to make the human race strong enough to withstand the coming Ido merge. "They gonna know somethin's happenin' in New York 'cause'a all that blue energy they see. Maybe they figured out how to track the crystal wings. We got to get out of here and start a movement. I'm gonna go to California and take a job in the prison system. I'll get with prisoners about to be released and offer them power."

"How will you hide their Ido?" I asked.

"We can change our shape temporarily," Cylla said. "We can become crystal wings for a while once more after the second transition."

"I'll flood the West Coast with an army of Ido men," Frank said. "My army in turn will go to their brothers and sisters in the hood and the gangs and make more. Some of these people will migrate down into Mexico and Central America, others will make their way home and to Africa."

It was we three black men in the inner circle making plans. Our gods, the Ido immortals, sat to the side understanding our intentions but unable to come up with them on their own. They were peaceful by nature and any form of subterfuge or plotting was as alien to them as they were to us.

"What about me, Frank?" Pete asked.

"How's your moms, Pete?" Frank replied.

"She calls me John after my father. All she do is sit on the couch all day thinkin' 'bout what used to be."

"Tell her to hold on to one of our Ido brothers, and after she transforms go down to your family in the South. Get a job in hospital and give the terminally ill the chance to live again."

Frank was thinking fast. He wanted to concentrate the human transition so that when the next phase began the world would be ready.

"Can two people merge with one'a your people at the same time?" Frank asked his wolf.

"Yes," Gorda replied. It seemed that Frank and Yaw had a sympathetic relationship where they understood each other but the human-Ido answered so that we could all

understand. "If two people at once touch us they will transform as the Cleet or the Necrom Ant."

"So you could do couples," Frank told Pete. "Old people watchin' each other die ready to make the move."

"What about me, brother?" I asked.

"You the Prime One, Rexford," Frank said to me. "I cain't tell you what to do."

The wolf licked my hand then.

"You're the strategist, Frank. You are my choice."

"I got a plan between me and Pete," Frank said. "We'll turn people in the South and West but who knows . . . we might get caught at any time . . . either one or both of us. You need to come up with another plan that we don't know about. Another plan that will be our fail-safe."

Silence filled the room. I could hear the thoughts of my friends, new and old. I could see what they felt and dreamed and feared. The experience was inhuman, exquisitely so. We didn't talk or even articulate in our minds; there was just a time of reflections and reverberations that passed between us like echoing waves forming complex geometric patterns across the lake of our lives.

The phone rang. It rang many times.

"Hello?" I said into the receiver.

"Is Frank there, Raleigh?" Hilda asked.

"Right here, Hildy."

Frank got on the line and said all of the right words. He told Hilda that I was going to lend him some money and that they were going out to California to start a new life. He promised to be home soon.

"And, oh yeah," Frank said as an afterthought, "I got me a dog."

After that Pete and Gorda and Frank and Yaw left us. There were no embraces or heroic nods. They just went their ways, the plan in their minds.

"You are a strange life-form," Cylla said to me when we were alone.

"Because we fight?"

"Because of the vacuum in your being," she said. "There is something so beautiful and so desolate about earthly life. You live alone for a short while that seems like all the time in the world and then you simply cease to be. Each life bound for such sadness and yet you survive."

She touched my face with her fingertips and I felt her as humans feel. I could see the beauty in my brief, insignificant life. Cylla's being was monumental and eternal. She was the god-mind come to a mortal plane. But I was the savior, the chance occurrence that was also humanity's only hope. I was nobody but for a coin toss, a flittering current of solar energy that brought Cylla to my room rather than Mr. Cram's den on the floor above.

"I love you," I said, a man talking to the stars.

IN MY SLEEP I knew her there next to me: a thousand thousand years at the crossroads from land to sea in the Ido world. Billions reached out to her for knowledge or to tell of their journeys. There were mishaps and misunderstandings but there was no war, no murder, no race.

I curled up into a fetal ball and she wrapped around me, loving me as an earthly woman would try to do.

———

IN MY SLEEP I heard hard crass sounds; knocking, pounding. Now and then there was a scream or shout but I would not awaken for anything. The dream that was Cylla's long history kept my attention tight like the skin of an apple, like the ocean across the Earth. The ecstasy of my fragility made everything else inconsequential.

It wasn't until our door was broken in that I was roused.

A dozen men in suits and men and women in army uniforms flooded my apartment. They invaded my bedroom, pulled Cylla and I naked from our bed.

Panic flushed in my heart. I felt Frank and Pete responding to my fears. For a moment I could see them both in different places. Hilda was packing as Frank stroked his wolf's thick fur and Pete was standing next to his mother as she was being pierced by the white teeth of yet another Ido immigrant.

"Identification!" the man standing in front of me shouted. I was dimly aware that he had asked the question more than once.

He was wearing thick glasses like Frank wore the day before—what seemed like years ago. His suit was black but not formal. There was a holster under the jacket and a gun butt protruding.

My inquisitor was white but many of his soldiers were black and brown men and women, moving like the Necrom Ants of Mali, searching (even if they didn't know it) for evidence of intergalactic espionage.

"Put on some pants!" the white man screamed, pushing me, knocking me down to the floor.

"You just woke him up, mothahfuckah!" Cylla shouted.

While I dreamed of her magnitude she had been studying the minutiae of my negligible existence. I was so excited
by this that I hurried on my pants so that the assembled rep-
resentatives of the government didn't witness my burgeoning erection.

While I hustled on my pants Cylla, our blanket wrapped
snugly around her, reached into her new pants pocket and
came out with a simple folded paper pamphlet. The front
had some letters scrawled on it that I couldn't quite make
out. When the white man opened the little, passport-
sized, booklet I spied a small photograph of Cylla. She was
smiling.

The white man thumbed through the pages as I took out
my wallet and searched for my driver's license. While I
fumbled I wondered what to do. Cylla had no real identification. Maybe she'd assembled the little booklet thinking
that a picture on a piece of paper was ID enough.

"Thank you, Miss Bene," the man said handing her back
the poor counterfeit.

He held out his hand to me and I gave him what I had.

He studied my valid license much more closely than he
did Cylla's fake papers. There were more than a dozen
people standing around us in the small bedroom by the time
he handed it back to me.

"Mr. Redman, have you noticed anything odd happening in your building?" he asked.

"Who are you?" Cylla said.

"Tanner," he said. "I work for the government. And we
believe that this so-called pole-snake phenomenon has centered on your neighborhood."

I gasped. Really—gasped. It's the only time I ever made that noise. For a moment I feared that my reaction would incriminate us—but I was wrong.

"I understand your fear," Agent Tanner said. "These things may be a threat to the entire world. The government hasn't decided whether they're a synthetic life-form or a weapon or both. We've blocked off the whole neighborhood and we're going to search every inch of this place before anybody or anything leaves."

"Don't they explode?" I asked.

"Only if they're cornered. Our scientists have come up with a containment plan."

A soldier came up and whispered in Tanner's ear.

"The upstairs neighbor," Tanner said and then he turned to his information officer. The soldier whispered again and Tanner continued. "A man named Cram . . . he says that there's been a lot of noise down here at all times of the day and night."

"Well," I said trying to seem as if I were embarrassed, "Cylla and I just met a little while ago and I guess, I guess we get a little carried away sometimes. Two in the afternoon, two at night . . . A couple'a times we even had some friends over. I guess we should apologize."

"Don't you go to work, Mr. Redman?"

"No, sir."

"Unemployed?"

"Kind of. I won the big lotto a while ago. I don't do nobody's work no more."

This revelation shocked Tanner off any road that might lead to pole-snakes. I mean, how could a guy win the lot-

tery *and* receive alien visitors from another galaxy, another universe?

Tanner stared at us a moment. There were questions in his mind; I could feel them but they did not make themselves evident. My Ido perceptions experienced his intellect as garbled, angry.

"Have you heard or seen anything strange, Miss Bene?"

"No. But it's like Rahl said . . . we've just been together."

Tanner was stymied. We were lovers, rich, young, even beautiful. He was on the hunt for monsters. He stood to the side while the soldiers searched my small apartment from top to bottom. After they were finished a small black man in a green suit, wearing overlarge glasses came in carrying a small handheld device. There were different varied colored lights and buttons on the PDA–like device.

The diminutive agent walked up to me pressing buttons and interpreting light patterns.

My response was deep dread. Maybe the government had come up with some way of identifying Ido. After a moment of study he turned to Cylla. She scowled at the man the way a young black woman from the hood might but there was no fear in her face.

"What's that?" I asked, no longer able to restrain my fears.

"It's just a device," the little agent said. "It tells us where the creatures have been."

He studied Cylla for a long time. When he was finished he took Tanner into a corner where they huddled for what seemed like half an hour.

Finally the white agent looked up and gestured at his

small army. They began filing out of the room. Cylla and I
followed them into the living room. The furniture had been
moved around but Cylla and Gorda had cleaned up the
blood.

Tanner and his small black technician were the last to go.

"What's this all about?" I asked him. "I mean, should we
be moving out of the neighborhood?"

"No, not at all," he said. "The radiation, as far as we
can tell, is harmless. We're looking for more intense read-
ings. Don't worry, Mr. Redman, we'll find what we're after.
You just call 911 if you see anything."

"SHOW ME YOUR IDENTIFICATION," I said to Cylla after
Tanner and his forces were gone.

She held out a simple paper diary purchased in some
high-end stationery store. There were symbols something
like letters and simple forms scribbled across the flimsy
cover and the ensuing pages. On the first page was a Pola-
roid photograph of her rudely taped down. The only rec-
ognizable letters were written in a child's scrawl underneath
the photograph: CYLLA BENE.

"Where'd you get the picture?"

"Gorda and I met a man with a camera that made instant pictures. We kissed him and he gave us each a photograph."

"But this is nonsense," I said slapping the insubstantial
faux document.

"Not to a lesser mind looking for monsters."

As if trying to prove our story Cylla and I spent the next few days in bed. Frank and Pete along with Mrs. Tingle, Pete's mother, and Hilda and Yaw all left the city while I taught Cylla different ways of kissing and she showed me how to inhale the stars with my being.

Tanner and his bosses and minions knocked in doors and turned over trash cans, crawled through the sewers and asked questions with no potential to understand.

"Will your whole world come here?" I asked Cylla as she washed the dishes and I caressed her from behind. We were both naked and sated, waiting for the blockade to come to an end or the passion to rise in us again.

"No. No one wants to leave but we feel that our essence would be lost if we all stayed to fight the gray cold. Four million of us will come to your home during the second and last phase of our migration. There will be a few others that will attempt to merge with other worlds."

I kissed the back of her neck and she sighed.

Frank was already in California. I could enter the mind of Yaw almost at will. It was an unsettling and a satisfying experience becoming the wolf watching her master.

"There is no vessel too small," Cylla said leaning back against me.

"What?"

"It is the oldest creed of my race," she said. "The simplest life of the smallest creature is magnificent and impossibly complex."

"Why are you saying this to me?"

She turned, crossing her arms behind my neck. The dishwater dripped down the small of my back onto my buttocks and thighs.

"Because it is so hard for you to understand the images," she said. "You are related to every life-form on this planet but your isolation makes you feel different. Your greatness is hidden from your awareness and so I must tell you nursery stories to make you begin to understand."

WHEN THE BLOCKADES around Gramercy Park came down I went with Cylla to get my father's classic pink Ford Galaxie 500. We drove for four days finally making it to western Canada, about a hundred miles north of Vancouver. We parked the car by the side of the road in the middle of a great forest.

From there we made our way into the woods.

I wasn't much of an outdoorsman before that time. I'd never been on a camping trip, spent the night in a sleeping bag, or built a fire in the woods. But Cylla and I lived in nature, with a few provisions we carried. It was summer and warm enough. And Cylla loved the trees.

"They're so beautiful and wise," she said as we clambered over ancient roots. "They soar and hug the earth."

"Call one of your people now, Cylla," I said.

Her grin was gleeful. She raised both hands and I felt something . . . it was like a piece of cinematic music telling of an approach. The sky seemed to lighten and a subtle radiance formed above our heads.

"Did you come to me like this?" I asked.

"Yes," she said.

It was midmorning in the woods and birds were singing.

"Why didn't I see this light, sense your approach?" I asked.

"You have learned something," she said and a sparkle occurred between her upheld hands.

The Ido bundle came down out of nowhere, a wavering, upstanding branch of some dead tree hissing and vibrating in the morning of a new world.

Cylla placed the quivering branch next to a huge tree, what is known as a grand fir, which loomed over two hundred feet above us. It was thick and old, crowned with green like a forest denizen should be. The Ido bundle's "teeth" reached out and touched the big tree. It was a feathery touch. The bundle trembled and then fell into the huge fir. The ground around us quaked as the needles of the great tree rattled and hissed.

"The tree has accepted us," Cylla said but I already knew that.

"Can you tell it to call down a thousand other bundles?" I asked.

"So many?"

"And all at the same time," I said. "All around here for a hundred miles. That way there will be a refuge for the Ido if things go bad."

Cylla nodded she concentrated for only a moment and then nodded again.

"It's done," she said.

"So quickly?"

"One or a billion and one," she said. "It's all the same."

She grabbed my hand and we were off knowing that Tanner or someone very much like him would soon be in the great northwest looking for pole-snakes and rousting mountain lions.

"*WHAT NEXT?*" *CYLLA ASKED.*

"Maybe we can start with other animals," I said. "Mountain lions, beavers."

"You don't only want humans?"

"No."

"Why not? In your mind isn't humanity the highest form of life?" Cylla was developing a wry sense of humor.

"Oceanus," I said in a somber tone.

The killer blue whale had destroyed a hundred fishing vessels by then. He had fathered a pod of militant whale ecologists.

"Dolphus empowered Oceanus because he knew that the world needed him," I said.

I felt then that I was at the last moment of prehistory. The world was about to begin. Humans and ants, whales and woodlands would realize, each in his own way, the possibility within and without.

I felt that I was outside in the dark of a doorway looking into a brightly lit world. We were in the grandeur of that magnificent forest and I hesitated in my mind, savoring the last moments of my animal ignorance.

CYLLA AND I MADE OUR WAY back to the car. I started it up and we drove south. Dimly I wondered if we might take over some zoo, bringing Ido bundles to elephants and tigers, rattlesnakes and frogs.

In the nights I had dreamed of Oceanus; the great blue whale stalking the slaughterers of fish. His Ido familiar

was a small mutated fish that could sense the coming of danger. I felt the power of the behemoth as he fought for the life of the ocean. Humanity needed allies like Oceanus. I knew that when Frank called up his wolf.

WE HAD MADE IT to the border after a few hours. Cylla and I held hands all the way. She was a billion years of enlightened experience and I was a fleeting moment of awareness that caught her fancy. We were as unlikely as justice among men, as spoken language from a newborn—but this only served to make us more real. The originality of our union stood out across two universes and made me both blind and nearly deaf.

"That's him!" someone shouted. I looked out of the window and saw Tanner and three dozen heavily armed soldiers racing toward us.

ENLIGHTENMENT IS A RELATIVE THING. A Neanderthal seeing fire and imaging its use is no less miraculous than a Buddhist master sitting beneath the Bodhi Tree and seeing for the first time that all things are one.

I'd experienced forms of enlightenment my entire life: speaking my first word without a stutter; touching Cylla's bundle and coming to myself; seeing her become the woman I had never known I needed; and becoming a traitor to my species in order to save them.

When Cylla and I were waiting on line in my father's car, holding hands with a world of knowledge being passed between us, I was being opened like a fig, like a cursed tomb,

like an infection that needed to drain. The depth of this experience was similar to a baby looking up to see his mother sigh or a Cleet breaking through its blue-green shell.

Behind us I could feel the transformation of a thousand Ido wings becoming bundles and merging with our forest, changing life forever. I felt exhausted by my labors and the ideas that sliced through me.

So when Tanner shouted and ran at us I had no strength to respond. They yanked open the car doors and pulled us out onto the asphalt of the highway.

Cylla fought bravely. She threw one man at least eight feet and knocked two more to the ground. Four large soldiers tried to restrain her but she tossed them off like children. Then more men came at her with truncheons.

"Don't kill her!" Tanner cried.

They beat her senseless. I tried to move to her side but I was held down by three or four brawny soldiers.

Two coffin-sized aluminum canisters were brought out and we were each bunged into them.

Just before they closed the seal Cylla's mind reached out to me.

"You and I are one and the same here and elsewhere. Do not fear for you have saved your people as I have saved mine. We may not survive but . . ."

And then the seal was set in place and I was completely alone for the first time in many days.

THEY MUST HAVE RELEASED a sedative in my container. I passed out, awoke, and passed out again. In my dreams I was searching for Cylla. She was everything to me. She was

my heart and my history. She was my hope and I knew that somewhere she was wanting me.

I AWOKE ON MY BACK in a cage that was three feet wide, six and half feet long, and only eighteen inches high. Those might not have been the exact proportions but that estimate is close enough. There was the stench of unwashed men all around me; they were confined in similar cages. The sun was beating down and there were snatches of conversations in Arabic being spoken now and then. There were other languages too.

I was clad in a pair of green cotton trousers and the sun was hot on my skin. The air was not only rank and hot but also humid and heavy.

I could not feel Cylla anywhere in the world.

Frank was busy transforming a man into an Ido in the back room of a small house somewhere. The police had come after him in California but his wolf saved him.

Pete and his mother, now transformed into a young woman, were traveling with Gorda and a man named Fixx, Mrs. Tingle's Ido familiar, in a Christian revival show that worked in a big tent like a circus. The police had come after them but they too had gotten away.

The Cleet were building an aerie while huge, mutated Necrom Ants excavated thousands of miles of tunnels.

Oceanus had been killed by a B-52 bomber but his children were well on their way to continuing his mission.

I was nauseous and in pain but that didn't matter. The loneliness in my heart was so overwhelming that I cried and cried for days.

No one had brought me food or water that first day and night.

Parched, I swam through the oceans. Fevered, I crawled in darkness excavating in the ecstatic scents of my sisters and the promise of Ido. Weak, I felt the hard ground beneath me, holding me up.

"Brother. Brother," a man said.

"Yes?" I answered unable to see where the question came from.

"You were talking out of your head," the man said in a thick Arabic accent. "Are you American?"

"Yes."

"Do they say you are Jihad?"

"They think I'm an alien from another planet or something," I said.

I was no longer with the children of Oceanus or the sharp-eyed Cleet. Now I was just a man dealing with the lies and tricks of my race.

"Are you crazy?"

"They're the crazy ones. I'm just in love with a girl."

"Is she from space?"

"I'm sure they think so."

I LAY FOR DAYS, weeks in my wire cage. Every other day I got water and unsweetened, chalky pudding. I became delirious not knowing if Cylla was a dream or some fantasy; if Oceanus's children were hallucinations or portents.

Once every third day they came out with hoses and washed us down with a powerful, painful spray.

Time passed and I stopped wondering. Images flitted before me—no more than dreams. I couldn't hold on to them.

I thought of Mr. Slatkin in his small bookstore, remembering his aged father pushing a cart through the streets of the old Lower East Side. I could hear them speaking Yiddish as I could hear and glimpse the Arabic dreams around me. We were writhing in hell but it wasn't so bad. It could have been worse: I might never have known the beauty of unity.

One day they got me from my soiled cage and dragged me into a yard where I was hosed down with frigid water. The shock of the cold sent a violent shiver through my weakened frame and I collapsed.

When I woke up I was seated in a chair in a one-room wooden hut. There was a powerful light shining in my eyes.

"Raleigh Rexford Redman?" a Voice demanded from the deep shadows beyond the light.

I knew that I should answer him but I didn't have the strength to speak.

From the right someone struck me with something hard. I felt the force of the blow but neither my scalp nor skull registered the pain. I yelped and fell though. Two men dragged me back to the chair and dropped me there.

"What's the date?" I asked.

"Are you Raleigh Rexford Redman?"

"Nobody calls me Rexford," I said into the shadows, "except sometimes Frank when he's foolin' around."

I was struck again but this time I did not fall.

"Are you Raleigh Rexford Redman?"

"Yes."

Now the pain was blossoming at the side of my head.

Looking down I noticed that my wrists were frighteningly thin.

"We know that your girlfriend has been infected by the pole-snake."

I remembered when the news anchor had made up the name. It seemed funny to me that the government would officially adopt the appellation. I guess I laughed.

I was struck again and decided to put away my humor.

"Did she force you to go with her?" the Voice boomed.

"I love her."

"What were you doing in Canada?"

"Camping."

"We've seen the charts," the man said. "There must be a thousand of those things in the woods."

"I wouldn't know about that, sir," I said lamenting and rejoicing in my human ability to prevaricate.

I was hit again. This time I fell down and out.

The next thing I knew extraordinarily cold water was being poured on me. It was shocking because the air was so hot.

"Where is Cylla from?" the Voice asked.

Again I knew I should answer but this time I couldn't because I was shivering. My teeth chattered and my hands unwillingly clenched into fists. I could feel the man on my right getting ready to strike me again.

"Wait," the Voice said, and the blow did not come.

I felt deeply grateful to the Voice that had held back the blow.

"Can you speak, Mr. Redman?"

"N-n-n-no, no," I stuttered.

"Take your time."

For a moment or two more I trembled and then, when the shivering passed, I began to sweat again. I nodded.

"Where is Cylla Bene from?" the Voice asked.

"I met her in a bar, in Chelsea. I told her that I was rich on account'a I won the lottery and she and me got tight."

"You told Nicci Charbon that Cylla was from another country, that her family was in trouble and wanted to emigrate."

"Where are we?" I asked.

"Guantanamo naval base . . . in Cuba."

"That was a metaphor," I said.

"Metaphor? What metaphor?"

"Something that perfectly describes the essence of something else," I said. "Cylla's love for me made her want to leave everything behind. And that's how I feel about her."

"She only cares about you because of your money," the Voice said.

"That's a metaphor too."

I sensed something then. I turned to my right and saw the soldier, a blond-haired woman, thrusting the butt of her rifle at my forehead.

WHEN I AWOKE I was in a hospital bed. A man was doing something to my skull, drilling. I cried out and fainted.

I WOKE UP in the hot Cuban night, back in my coffin cage. I could smell my fellow man, hear his convulsions and labored breaths. There were prayers being chanted and curses all around.

I thought that if this was the worst they had to offer that it wasn't too bad.

TWO OR THREE DAYS later they came and got me again. I had spent most of that time drifting in and out of consciousness. That's why I was so unsure about how much time had passed.

I was taken to a small lime-green room that smelled of disinfectant. The room was furnished with two wooden chairs and a metal table. They sat me in a chair that had leather manacles on the arms and legs. The blond woman sergeant strapped me in while an infantryman held a pistol to my head.

The room was cold. It had air-conditioning. At first it was a relief to be out of the heat but after a while the cold began to hurt my bare hands and feet.

The two soldiers flanked me, not speaking or sitting or even talking to each other. We'd been like that for quite a while, an hour or more, before the green metal door opened and a man in fancy combat clothes stalked in. There was a star on his dark green helmet and a pistol on his hip. In his left hand he carried a small hatchet with a dark haft.

Before sitting down behind the table in front of me the officer handed the hatchet to the blond sergeant. She took it without comment or hesitation.

This officer sat down and stared at me. I looked him in the eye trying to come up with the power I called upon to send Tom Beam into convulsions. But it didn't work.

"What is this thing you put in my head?" I asked the nameless soldier.

"You have some radiation in your body," he said easily. "The node emits a pulse that nullifies it as far as we can tell."

The seated officer was in his fifties, white (as were the two other soldiers), with weathered skin. He was powerful looking with as unsympathetic a visage as I had ever beheld.

After a minute he turned his gaze to the woman and nodded.

While I was looking at her the infantryman grabbed my right hand and held it so that only my baby finger was sticking out. The woman, who I will always think of as Blondie, then made a quick motion and lopped that finger off.

I screamed. I shouted and jerked around making the chair hop in front of the stone-faced military men and woman. Blood spurted from the finger stump but they didn't say anything, didn't ask me anything.

When I had quieted down, the officer said to Blondie, "Another."

"No! Stop!"

They chopped off the three fingers of my right hand leaving me only with the thumb and index finger. I passed out after the last disfigurement. When I awoke I was in the cage again.

"Brother," a man nearby called to me. "I will pray for you."

I remember thinking that I was a member of the democracy that had tacitly agreed to imprison and torture this man. His generosity tore at my heart.

I fell unconscious and awoke in a hospital bed set in the corner of a cluttered and cramped sickroom. My right hand was half the size of a football and it hurt so terribly that I cried out.

I was sorry for the outburst when the officer that had ordered my amputations came into the messy room.

"You're awake," he said.

"I'm dying."

"No, son. There's a long way between a swollen hand and death."

"Half a hand."

"You're lucky I let you keep that."

I smiled then. Ever since the head operation I had been cut off from any connection with Ido consciousness. The metal stud implanted in my skull seemed to be vibrating; and then for a flash I saw the Necrom Queen, a huge-bodied creature in a great chamber a thousand feet below the desert. She looked like a rainbow, hardly an insect-form at all, dropping creatures of all colors and forms moving under the sand, preparing for the Merge.

The image was gone and so was the pain in my hand. My Ido vision subsided but I was satisfied.

"What are you grinning about, punk?" the nameless officer said.

"You're an evil man," I replied. "You study evil but you think it's gonna turn out good. That's why I'm laughing. Because I know that you're a fool."

"I need to know about Cylla Bene, her people, and their plans," he said. "We believe that either the Mongolians or the North Koreans, or both are responsible for these creatures. We need for you to help us prove this or you will see evil like even Hitler's brightest stars couldn't imagine."

————

I COULD DETAIL more of this very early part of the Greater History of Earth but it would be pornographic in its depiction of violence. And there's no need. I never found out my torturer's name or exact rank. I lost my right hand, my testicles, left leg to the hip, and right leg to the knee. They gouged out my left eye, both ears were hacked from my head, and they cut off the baby finger of my left hand— I'm not sure why they did that. I was rarely given any kind of painkiller and it took a whole staff of doctors and nurses to keep me alive. Months passed and I was made to suffer in a thousand ways. They wanted to know about Pete and Frank and Cylla and even old Mr. Slatkin.

I never answered. When the pain got too great I was visited by the vision of the Necrom Queen and experienced relief for a while. Somehow the ants had found a way around the stud the army used to negate the blue radiance of Ido.

Months went by. There was one nurse, a black woman named Carla, who prayed over me and asked me to forgive her . . .

ONE DAY THE VOICE CAME into my hospital–torture room with six soldiers. They lifted all seventy-five pounds of me from the bed, threw me on a cot, and carried me to a helicopter. I threw up from motion sickness in the whirlybird. Carla had to turn me on my side so that I didn't drown in my own vomit.

We came to an airbase where I was put on a jet. I was flown to Washington, D.C., and transferred by ambulance to an underground bunker filled with men and women in lab coats and uniforms, suits and street clothes.

They took me to a darkish chamber where there was a huge conference table with mostly men, and a few women, sitting around. I was rolled in on a kind of stripped-down utility wheelchair. The stump of my right leg was bleeding through the bandages and the socket from my missing eye oozed pus down my bony cheek. Because I only had one eye I had to keep moving my head to see the assembled inquisitors.

"Mr. Redman," said a black woman who was sitting at the head of the table.

I had been positioned at the foot of the table.

"Yes. Yes, I'm Redman." It was hard for me to catch my breath. I suspect that I had developed some kind of lung disease or infection.

There were three large screens behind the speaker. They came to life the moment I spoke.

"Are you familiar with the term 'Ido'?" the woman asked. She was dark skinned and smallish with a hard body and intelligent and cold eyes that reminded me of the Cleet.

I was stunned even in my state of dissolution. I opened my mouth but there was nothing to say.

On the screens behind the woman images had begun to appear. It was hard for me to make them out because my one eye started tearing when I stared too long. On the leftmost monitor there was an image of an island floating in the sky above the ocean. There were large aircraft carriers below this airborne landmass, they seemed like toys compared with the size of the mountain hovering above them.

The plasma screen on the right side showed a city made of semitransparent, multicolored spirals that sat in the middle of a great sand-covered expanse. The center image was of a

huge mound of branches, leaves, and other plant material rising like a mountain out of a dense green forest.

Slowly I began to understand what the images meant. The Ido had come to Earth and set up three cities, four if you counted the silent forests of the great Northwest. The Cleet, the offspring of Dolphus, the Necrom and their Queen had called forth their familiars.

"Mr. Redman."

"What's your name?"

"Cordelia Martin," she said, "the Under Secretary of State."

"Huh."

"Do you know the term 'Ido'?" she said slowly, threateningly.

"Miss Martin, you can see what your people have already done to me. I've been amputated, emasculated, tortured, and spit on. So you can take that tone right outta your voice. I'm not afraid of you."

"Mr. Redman," Cordelia said, modulating her tone. "This is a worldwide threat. The Russians, French, and Chinese are preparing nuclear attacks on each of these places. The safety of every man, woman, and child in the world may be in your hands."

"I only have one hand, ma'am."

That brought complete silence to the room. Everyone there realized how far they'd gone and how close they'd come to being lost.

"We were unaware of your treatment at Guantanamo, Mr. Redman," said a man in a dark suit sitting to my left.

I didn't answer him.

After a few more moments of silence I said, "Where is Cylla Bene?"

"She is none of your concern," Ms. Martin informed me.

"Then drop your A-bombs and shoot me too because if I don't see Cylla you don't get shit from me."

"We can destroy these, these manifestations," Martin said.

"No," I said, "you can't. You don't even understand them. Your whole world will fall into ashes before you even have a notion of what you're facing."

"Cylla Bene has been designated a national threat," the white man in the dark suit said.

"Bring her to me or see the human race fall into ruin," I proclaimed.

"What does the term 'Ido' mean?" another man asked. He was on my right side so I didn't see him because I was concentrating on Cordelia.

"It means the transformation of men into angels . . . or corpses depending on if you allow me to see Cylla or not."

While we spoke a nuclear bomb went off over the South American aviary. The mushroom cloud and the decimation of the surrounding forest was immediate and ongoing. The trees for many miles burned and fumed. For long minutes the explosion unfolded, deepened, destroying life for a hundred-mile radius. It must have been a hydrogen bomb, the product of man at his lowest.

When the smoke began to clear it became obvious that the Mound Aerie had survived—completely intact.

The silence that consumed the room when the bomb went

off was replaced by an agitated din of fear. A man ran at me, knocking me from the wheelchair.

"Bastard!" he shouted. "Motherfucker!"

He kicked me and fell upon me throwing punches and making gurgling sounds in his throat.

Two soldiers pulled him off me but no one moved to put me back in the wheelchair. I was hemorrhaging from my knee and head. The metal stud that had been anchored to my skull popped out and a plethora of indecipherable images came into my mind. I felt dizzy. The room became hazy and I passed from awareness almost into unconsciousness— then I entered a limbo state.

"Rahl?" Pete said or thought or felt.

"Hey, man. Where are you?"

"I'm here with Frank. We're in this podunk town in northern Idaho. We got people all over the Northwestern states with their Ido. We're waitin' for you, brothah."

"I don't know, Pete. They done cut me down pretty bad. Can't walk, half blind . . . I don't know if I'm'onna make it."

"You got to make it, man," Pete said. "You the Prime One for the human race. Without you there's no connection."

"What if I die?"

"Then the few of us who merged will make it but everybody else will be on their own."

Pete faded away and Cylla came to mind. I could see her in my memory. I loved her so much that I knew I wouldn't give up on her even for all the people in the world.

When I opened my eyes again I was in a chair in a room sitting across from the president of the United States. I hadn't voted for him . . . really, what I mean is I wouldn't have voted for him if I had voted.

"Mr. Redman," the white man in the blue suit said.

"Yeah?"

"We need to figure this out." He was affable but I could see the coldness in his eyes.

"Bring me Cylla and I will save your world," I said more like a conqueror than an invalid.

"She has been hurt," he said, a hint of apology in his voice.

"You tortured her?"

"We were trying to save the world."

"Where is she?"

THEY CREATED AN ENTIRE STRUCTURE to house Cylla. I later found out that some Brazilian physicist named Parde had developed a device that could read with accuracy where the Blue Radiance (later known as "Ido Essence") had occurred most deeply. When they used this machine on Cylla they figured that she was one of the mutating pole-snakes that came either from Mongolia or North Korea, or both.

The building was made from glistening metal and was kept on a huge and abandoned army base in Virginia. It was mound shaped, three stories high, glistening in the sun like a religious icon dedicated to the female breast.

I was wheeled through the front door that led to a four-tiered chamber that went around the whole inside of the building. There were at least a hundred technicians and the like sitting at desks on every tier looking at monitors of various types.

"Where is Cylla?" I asked the president.

He was walking beside my chair as his aide pushed me along.

"She's in a room at the center of the building," another person said, a woman in a lavender dress wearing a necklace of multicolored gems. "We have isolated her because of the explosions that occurred in Mongolia and Russia."

"You think this structure could contain an explosion like that?" I asked the woman.

"It could contain a tactical nuclear device," she said with certainty.

Science, I thought, had come a long way in the deep shadows cast by the Patriot Act and the subsequent victory of terrorism.

"I want to see her," I said.

We had come to a door where a tall Hispanic man stood. He was dark-skinned with Asiatic eyes. He wasn't burly but there was strength in his stand. From my recent experiences I recognized him as a torturer.

For a moment I panicked thinking that I had been brought to this place to be persecuted further by this tall, heartless man.

"This is Luna," the woman in violet said. "He will take you in to your friend. But remember, we don't have much time. There is fear around the world over these manifestations. Either you tell us what Ido means or there will be a world war."

Luna moved to take my chair but I held up my one deformed hand to stop him.

"Why do you keep asking me about this word?" I asked the president.

He looked at me with his beady eyes and meaningless smirk. He glanced at the violet woman and hunched his shoulders.

The woman gave him a look, wordlessly referring to an earlier discussion.

"Tell me," I said.

The president made a decision then. His smirk turned into a grimace and he looked down on me: the half-man in the utility wheelchair.

"The mound in Brazil," he said, "it spoke to us."

"In English?"

"No, I mean I don't know. It said the word 'Ido' over and over again and then, the next day, it said your name."

"Raleigh Redman?"

"Yeah. Do you know why?" The president wasn't actually a fool. I could see in his eyes that he had the ability to understand the basic nature of people.

"No," I said not caring if he believed me or not. "But I can talk to Cylla about it. She'll talk to me."

The metal door in front of us slid open on that cue. Luna pushed me into a small metal chamber, the door behind us closed, the door before us opened, and we went through.

We passed through seven doors until we got to a moderate-sized all-white room with a bed at the center. Upon this bed with no sheet or pillow or blanket lay what was left of Cylla Bene.

Her limbs were amputated at the elbows and knees and the skin of what was left of her arms and legs was scorched and close to the bone. Her hair was gone as were her lips and ears and eyes. There was blood on the mattress and on the floor around the bed.

"Leave me," I said to Luna.

"It's all right, Luna," a voice said over loudspeaker.

"Rahl?" Cylla called in the yawning pronunciation that the lack of articulating lips allowed.

I heard the door behind me slide open and then shut.

It was with great difficulty that I shifted in my chair to make certain with my one eye that the torturer was gone.

"Rahl?" Cylla cried.

"Yeah, baby," I said. "I'm here."

I reached out with my one hand and clutched the edge of the mattress. I pulled until I was flush with the side of her bed.

"I'm here," I said.

"I was just dreaming of you," she said, unable to make a satisfactory "m," "j," or "f" sound.

"You must have known I was coming."

"I always dream of you . . . of you."

She made a coughing sound then that I knew was her crying.

I lurched about and reached for the stump of her right arm. I missed the first time.

"Do not touch the prisoner," the amplified voice commanded.

I reached out again and grabbed on to the bony elbow joint.

It was at that moment I finally understood everything. The world as I had known it, even under the influence of Cylla's Ido consciousness, fell away . . .

"Release the prisoner immediately," the voice commanded but it was far too late to have any consequence for me or Cylla or the fate of humanity in general.

I was in a shimmering globe of light. Next to me was

Cylla. We were physically destroyed but our love was a great solace to us.

Outside the globe of light were Cleet and the children of Dolphus and Oceanus, Necrom Antwomen sniffing the earth about them and trees that reached for the sun.

"You could not reach them without me," I said with my mind.

"No," she said. I noticed then that her lips had grown back.

"I am one of the connections between the various tribes of Ido," I said. "Without me the forest and all the people Pete and Frank transformed would wither."

"They might live but their ability to infuse with others would become impotent."

"You mean their ability to merge?"

"No," she said. "Only the original Ido could merge and even they could only do it once," she paused, "or maybe twice with a lover."

I felt strands of her body enter through my hand.

There were sounds all around us. The Cleet and Necrom and sea beings cheered. Pete and Frank began their northward journey with nearly nine thousand humans and their Ido familiars. The voice on the loudspeaker was screaming.

"We have not come to conquer," Cylla told me, "but to live and learn."

"Maybe we can help you defeat the gray coldness," I suggested.

My left arm had grown back. So had my legs.

The images of Ido around the globe faded as soldiers

invaded the room. They had automatic weapons raised to attack us. They opened fire. The bullets ceased to exist at the edge of our globe of light. Cylla was whole again. I was whole again. And we were surrounded by young men and women who were so frightened that they practiced murder in their hearts.

Oceanus II roared. He made a sound from his Pacific home that echoed around the world. Humans everywhere heard it subliminally. Some fell to their knees and cried; some leaped to their feet and shouted, "What was that?" But not only humans responded: birds and honey bees and ancient tortoises under the baked desert of Death Valley heard and felt a change in their souls.

The soldiers stopped shooting. Maybe they realized with that one bellowing note that Oceanus II had announced the end of the absolute reign of Man.

The sphere that surrounded us fell. We stood before the assembled troop of killers naked and beautiful in terms both Ido and human. Our connection was the final circuit that brought the Ido into our world completely.

Cylla took my hand and I sighed, relieved in hindsight that we had succeeded—if only barely.

The president sent the violet-clad woman in to talk to us.

"What does it mean?" she asked.

"The trees are growing in western Canada," I said.

The woman's face was slender and hard. Her eyes were dark topaz in color. She did not understand me.

"The trees are growing," I said again, "and moving too. They will form a fortress like the other alien cities. From inside those living walls humans will be called to merge with their predestined Ido familiars. Do not try to stop them."

"How many?" she asked.

"A million, no more."

"And do they intend to rule us?"

"No. They will bring us the gift of seeing differently."

"And what about the other cities?"

"They will each fill out their ranks and interact with all the life-forms on Earth. They will form into the way things will become."

"I don't understand," the woman said.

"Neither do I. The world of the Ido cannot exist here, not perfectly. And so we will come together and reach a . . . a biological compromise."

The woman was crying while the dry-eyed president hid somewhere. I could see that there would be upheaval throughout all the living kingdoms of the world. But as long as I had Cylla I could bear the changes.

WHEN WE GOT TO THE FORTRESS in the great Northwest I realized that almost all (but not all) of the original Ido had been hosted by black and brown peoples. North America had turned itself over to its conquered races and its slaves. Somehow that seemed right to me. We were the negation of the negation. Our job was to end their world and then to begin it.